A DARING DESIRE

THE DARE MÉNAGE SERIES
BOOK FOUR

JEANNE ST. JAMES

Jeanne
ST. JAMES

~

Editor: Proofreading by the Page

Cover Art: April Martinez

~

www.jeannestjames.com

Sign up for my newsletter for insider information, author news, and new releases:
www.jeannestjames.com/newslettersignup

❀ Created with Vellum

Warning: This book contains explicit scenes, some possible triggers and adult language which may be considered offensive to some readers. This book is for sale to adults ONLY, as defined by the laws of the country in which you made your purchase. Please store your files wisely, where they cannot be accessed by under-aged readers.

This is a work of fiction. Any similarity to actual persons, living or dead, or actual events, is purely coincidental.

Dirty Angels MC, Blue Avengers MC & Blood Fury MC are registered trademarks of Jeanne St James, Double-J Romance, Inc.

～

Keep an eye on her website at http://www.jeannestjames.com/or sign up for her newsletter to learn about her upcoming releases: http://www.jeannestjames.com/newslettersignup

Author Links: Instagram * Facebook * Goodreads Author Page * Newsletter * Jeanne's Review & Book Crew * BookBub * TikTok * YouTube

CHAPTER 1

G ryffin Ward's dick was so hard he winced.

The newest associate at his law firm stood on the other side of his desk talking. Actually *talking* to him.

He had no clue what she was even saying.

As he watched her lips move, he regretted hiring her. Even though she came highly recommended.

Rayne's stats were so good he would've been a fool not to. The more cases his practice won, the more clients they attracted. The more clients they drew, the larger his firm grew. Which meant—

Oh fuck. Who cared what it meant. Right now, he desperately needed to adjust himself because his erection was caught in his pants in a painful position.

"So, what do you think, Boss?"

Holy fuck with that "Boss" shit again.

She needed to start dressing like a nun and stop calling him that. Otherwise, he would have permanent blue balls.

What did he think? He didn't. All the blood in his brain had rushed to his dick, so he had no valid thoughts.

"You don't have to call me Boss. In fact, please don't."

"I know I don't." With a smile, Rayne leaned over and tapped him under the chin before spinning on the heel of her fuck-me pumps and heading toward the door. "But, I like it," she threw over her shoulder.

Me, too.

He took one last glance at her tight skirt with the slit in the back, the one that hugged her luscious ass and those stockings she wore with the line up the back of her legs, before she disappeared, leaving his office door open.

Gryff closed his eyes and blew out a breath.

Fuuuuuuuuuuuuuuuuck.

No wonder she won most of her cases. The judge and the ADA's brains were probably mush after watching her pace the courtroom cross-examining witnesses on the stand.

No matter what, she was highly respected for being a great defense attorney.

But, he should fire her. He didn't dip his pen in the company ink and he wasn't going to start now. Even though she sorely tempted him.

He was a wretch. That's what he was.

He blew out another ragged breath and scrubbed his hands over his face.

"Gryff," came a female voice from the door.

He separated his fingers enough to peer through them at his secretary, Dani. "Yeah?"

"Are you okay?"

Fuck no, he wasn't okay. He was completely jacked. "Yeah." He sighed and lowered his hands to his lap to cover the evidence, just in case she came closer.

"Okay, well, your brother is on line one."

If that didn't make his dick soften, then nothing would. "Thanks. Close the door, please."

She gave him a little smile and did as she was told. Now, there was a woman he could work with and not lose his mind. But then,

Dani dressed conservatively, like she actually worked in an office for a high-profile law firm. Unlike Rayne.

With a quick adjustment to his deflating manhood, he picked up the handset and jabbed the button for line one. "What's up, big brother?"

"Hey, what's up with you?" his older brother, Grae, returned.

If his brother only knew what had just been up.

Ever since Grae hooked up with his lovers, Paige and Connor, the man had definitely lost some of his stick-up-his-ass disposition and now sounded more relaxed. His proper English had relaxed a little bit, too. But then, Paige had a filthy mouth and cursed like a sailor, so it didn't surprise him that some of that rubbed off on Grae. It was about time his brother loosened up.

"I need a favor," Grae continued.

Damn. Grae never asked for anything. His squared-away older brother couldn't possibly be having any legal problems, could he?

"Shoot."

"I've got a player—"

Ah, fuck.

"That needs representation."

Another bad boy football player getting into a jam. Nothing new. However, Grae coming to him for help was.

"And you're the best."

Gryff frowned. "Are you trying to butter me up?"

"Yes. He needs your help. He's a great player and our team needs him, but he's been suspended until this little legal *snag* is cleared up."

"How little?"

"Minuscule."

"Bullshit."

"The judge wants to make an example out of him since he doesn't like professional athletes getting away with stuff like this."

Stuff like this. The words domestic and assault ping-ponged through Gryff's head. "Did he smack around his wife or girlfriend?"

"No."

"Stop beating around the bush, Grae. This isn't like you."

A pause came from the other end of the line.

"What's the charge?" Gryff prodded.

"Aggravated assault."

Gryff pursed his lips and leaned back in his leather office chair, staring up at the ceiling. "Who's the judge?"

"Thompkins."

Gryff sat up with a snap. *Shit.* He didn't want to hear the name of that hard-ass and he was pretty certain he didn't want to know the answer to the next question. "Who is it?"

"Trey Holloway."

Gryff closed his eyes and cursed silently. "No."

Trey Holloway had been in the news one too many times in the past few years. The guy seemed to be spinning out of control and it didn't surprise Gryff that he'd been charged with agg assault.

"It was self-defense."

"Sure it was." Gryff ground the heel of his palm into his right eye. He had the start of a blistering headache.

"I believe him," Grae said softly. "Look, I know the guy has some issues. He's a wild child, but he's good on the field. He's got potential to take us to the Super Bowl this upcoming season. I don't want to see him throw it away."

"Are you doing this for the team? Or for him?"

Another hesitation, then, "Both. One can help the other."

Maybe. But, a troublemaker on the team had the potential to make it implode, too. If anyone knew that, Grae should. And Gryff was sure he did know it. Why was Grae putting his neck on the line for this guy? Why was this guy different than any other player who got arrested for doing something stupid?

"Talk to me," Gryff said.

"He was at a bar—"

Yeah. That's how all the good stories began.

"And he came onto a guy—"

"He's gay?" Well, Gryff never expected that.

Grae ignored his question and continued, "They were outside behind the bar making out—"

Making out. Like teenagers?

"And the guy's friends caught them. When that happened, the guy accused Trey of forcing himself on him, since the guy wasn't out. The guy acts indignant and punches Trey to make the cover story look good. The guy's friends jump in, thumping on Trey, outnumbering him. But, Trey fights back and ends up taking all four guys down, injuring a couple of them pretty badly."

"Damn," Gryff whispered, picturing the whole thing in his head as his brother explained it.

"Right. But, it's Trey's word against the other four. No one else in the bar witnessed it and if they did, they haven't come forward. Trey claims it was self-defense and I believe him. No one in their right mind takes on four guys for the hell of it."

Unless they're drunk. "Was he the only one arrested?"

"He was the only one left standing in the end."

"Damn," Gryff whispered, again. "From what I've heard about him, you'd think Holloway would have a lawyer on retainer."

"He does. But this is life or death right now. Like I said, there's no one better than you."

"Life or death?"

"Of his career," Grae clarified.

Gryff spun his chair around to stare out of the window behind him. "Well, if that isn't some pressure..."

"You can handle it."

"I need some time to think about it."

"There's no time."

"Why? When is the—"

A throat cleared behind him. He looked over his shoulder and stared right into Trey Holloway's sky blue eyes. The guy gave him a wink and a cocky smile.

Get the fuck out of here.

"Grae," Gryff said in a menacing tone.

His brother chuckled. "I was going to warn you."

"Not fast enough."

"Yes, well—" and then the phone went dead.

Son of a bitch. He was going to kill his brother.

Gryff slowly turned his chair back around and carefully hung up the phone when he really wanted to smash it fifty times into the cradle until it exploded. But, he was civilized. He couldn't lose his shit in front of a client.

Even if it *was* Trey Holloway.

Gryff clearly needed to have a talk with Dani about letting clients just walk into his office without being announced or even invited in.

He studied the man standing in the middle of his office. His blue eyes looked lighter due to his dark tan. His dirty blond hair, streaked with highlights, whether fake or real, almost reached his shoulders. Scruff covered his jaw. The man was definitely built like a quarterback and not a linebacker. He wore a white button down shirt that emphasized his coloring, with the sleeves rolled up past his elbows and tucked into well-fitting jeans. Well-worn pointed cowboy boots covered feet that could move him downfield quickly when necessary.

"Like what you see?"

Gryff leveled his gaze at him. "I don't do men."

"Do they do you?"

Gryff pursed his lips and wondered if he should administer Trey's next ass whipping. Though, like the last time, it probably wouldn't do any good. He shook his head. "I don't swing that way."

"Never say never. Your brother does. Maybe it's in the genes."

Gryff's fingers clenched the arms of his office chair. So much for polite introductions. "You fuck a lot of men, Holloway?"

Trey quickly hid his surprise at the unexpected question. It was there one second and then gone the next, covered by the wide smile he plastered across his face. "You mean over my lifetime or in one night?"

Trey was trying to shock him, get a rise out of him. Two could play at that game.

"How many men have you had in one night?"

Trey lifted his hands up and spread his fingers. "I don't have enough fingers to count."

"If needed, you can use your toes, too."

The corners of Trey's lips twitched. "You've got a better sense of humor than your brother."

"You don't hear me laughing."

Then they flat lined. Trey studied Gryff for a moment then gave a sharp nod. "We got off on the wrong foot." He shoved his hand out. "Trey Holloway."

Gryff didn't take the offered hand nor did he even bother to glance at it. "I know who you are. Sit down."

Trey cocked an eyebrow but parked his ass in one of the seats meant for real clients. Not an irresponsible jackass like the one in front of him.

He propped his feet on Gryff's desk. *What. The. Fuck.*

"Get your filthy boots off my desk. Put your feet on the floor, sit up straight, and act like you have some sense."

Trey's feet dropped to the floor and he scooted back in the chair with sudden color in his cheeks. He cleared his throat. "Thanks for taking my case."

Now, it was Gryff's turn to cock a brow. "I didn't say yes, yet."

"I've been falsely accused."

"That's what the guilty always say."

"Hey, I was the victim."

"Sure."

Trey crossed his arms over his chest. "Your brother says you're the best."

"I am."

Trey hooked an ankle over his knee and smiled. "What's it going to take?"

"You keeping your ass clean and a five hundred-thousand-dollar retainer."

Trey's eyes widened and he whistled softly.

Ah, see? Two could play the shock and awe game. "If you fuck up, you lose the retainer."

"So, it's insurance."

"You catch on quickly."

Trey shook his head. "Just 'cause I play football doesn't mean I'm stupid."

"We'll see about that."

"Hey, Boss," Rayne burst in through the open doorway staring at a file as she walked, then stopped dead when she glanced up and spotted Trey. "Oh. Sorry. I didn't realize you were with anyone." Gryff didn't miss her green eyes widen when she recognized who sat in his office. "*Oh.*"

Yeah, *oh.*

Gryff's eyes narrowed as he watched her fingers brush over her hair, as if fixing it. There was nothing to fix, her long dark blonde hair always seems to have a 'just woke' look that fit her personality.

"You're Trey Holloway," she breathed.

Gryff frowned at the sudden color in her cheeks and the hungry look in her eyes.

Trey pushed himself to his feet and offered her his hand. Well, the guy may have some manners yet. "Yes, ma'am."

"Ma'am? Oh please." She almost giggled. *Giggled.* The corners of her lips curved as she curled her fingers around his.

Gryff's gaze glued to their hands. Hands that weren't shaking in greeting, just holding. Did his finger tickle her palm? Trey gave her a suggestive smile and raised her hand to his mouth, kissing her knuckles. "And you are?"

That seemed to jump start Rayne. "Oh, uh... Rayne. Rayne Jordan."

"Nice to meet you, Ms. Jordan."

"Uh, just Rayne." Holy shit, she just batted her eyelashes at him.

Gryff coughed loudly and both their heads spun toward him. "Holloway, take a seat. Rayne, what do you need?"

"Oh, it can wait, Boss."

She didn't move to leave. Oh, hell no. Instead, she moved to stand almost directly in front of Trey's chair and parked her ass on the edge of Gryff's desk. Just like that.

"Are you a new client?" Rayne asked Trey. Was she panting?

"Yes," he said, giving her a blinding smile.

Trey was the kind of guy who thought his looks and charm would get him through life. He needed a rude awakening. You'd think after getting arrested—and not for the first time—with a felony assault, a good ass kicking and then being suspended from the team, would have done it. Apparently not.

"We don't know yet," Gryff corrected. "We're still talking terms."

Without breaking eye contact with Rayne, Trey said, "There's nothing to talk about. I'll meet the terms."

A muscle in Gryff's jaw jumped. And jumped again. He was going to kill his brother.

CHAPTER 2

As soon as the door closed behind Rayne, Trey pinned him with his gaze. "Damn. Have you hit that?"

Gryff fought to keep his expression neutral. "Now, I see why you got your ass kicked."

"Hey, I held my own against four guys."

His apparent interest in Rayne made him wonder... "So, you like women, too?"

Trey gave a him a lazy shrug. "Why limit yourself to only half the population?"

Why indeed.

"I'm serious about these terms, Holloway. Keep your nose clean. I don't want to see you on the news. I don't want to even hear you made some woman cry. No drinking, no whoring, no fighting. Nothing. You will be an altar boy until this whole thing is over."

"Fine."

"And keep your dick out of my best attorney."

One side of Trey's mouth lifted. "You got dibs on her."

Gryff sighed. "No. But, if you fuck her then she can't represent you. So, I don't care if you have to jerk off a hundred times a day. Don't touch her."

"What if she touches me?"

Gryff raised an eyebrow and Trey lifted his hands in surrender.

"Okay. Okay. Nose clean. Dick zipped."

Gryff pushed himself to his feet. "Let's go."

With a curious look, Trey stood and followed him out of the office, past Dani's gaped and drooling mouth and down the hall. Stopping in front of Rayne's office door, he rapped a knuckle against it before pushing it open. Rayne looked up from her desk, looking sexy as hell and when she saw who was behind him, her eyes widened and her mouth made an O.

"Holloway's all yours," Gryff told her and shoved Trey into the room, shutting the door behind him.

Rayne was the best, and if anyone could get his charges dismissed, it was her. He didn't have the patience to deal with an irresponsible athlete himself. But damn, as he strode back to his office he couldn't shake the feeling he just made a big mistake.

~

"Boss?"

Rayne peeked around the partially open door of Gryff's office. It was late and the rest of the firm had cleared out like normal people.

She'd gotten tied up reading Trey's files and formulating a defense plan for the football player. Before she knew it, it was two hours past her normal quitting time.

She couldn't help that she had to surf the Internet "researching" her new client. Or stare at hundreds of pictures of the hot and handsome Trey Holloway. Some good, some downright delicious, and some bad, like his mugshots. Though, admittedly, he had still looked good in those. He wore a cocky smile in each one of them, as well.

The only light on in her boss's office was the one on his desk. The overhead fluorescents had been turned off and he leaned back in his chair, a hand covering his eyes. The knot in his tie had been pulled loose and the top button of his dress shirt undone. His suit jacket had been tossed over one of the chairs and his sleeves rolled up. This was the most skin she'd ever seen him show. His dark skin reminded her of a ripe plum. His forearms appeared solid and without his jacket on, she could see how broad his shoulders really were. This man needed no shoulder padding.

Rayne swallowed hard. Ever since joining his firm, she'd been fighting her attraction to him. Some of the other female associates said that he refused to play where he worked.

But, damn, the power that emanated from this man made her want him desperately. She pushed the door open wider, enough for her to slip through and then shut it quietly. She winced when the latch clicked, worried she'd disturb him.

Taking careful, quiet steps to his desk, she studied him. He wore no jewelry, only a gold watch that complimented his skin tone. She could see what looked like a dark tattoo peeking past one of his rolled-up sleeves.

The man had a tattoo? He seemed way too conservative for that. In the few months since she'd joined the firm, she never saw him dressed in anything but a suit and rarely without his jacket outside his own office.

"Boss?" she whispered again, not sure if she really wanted to disturb him. His fingers twitched over his eyes but there was no other reaction. Then he heaved a breath and sat straight up, pinning her in place with his dark gaze.

A frown marred his expression. "What are you doing in here?"

"I wanted to run something by you about the Holloway case."

He rubbed a hand down his face and then glanced at his watch. "It's late. You should go home. We can talk about it tomorrow."

"*You're* still here."

"I need to head home, too."

She wondered if anyone waited for him at home. The office rumor mill said no. That he lived alone and didn't even have a pet.

"Is that a tattoo?" she asked, tilting her chin toward his arm. *Oh, please say yes.*

He tugged at his sleeve self-consciously as if trying to hide it. "Rayne," he said, his voice a gentle warning.

"I'm just curious." *But, please, please say yes.*

One heartbeat, two. "Yes."

A fire ignited in Rayne's belly. And it wasn't because she'd eaten bad Mexican food. She tried to control the exhilaration in her voice. "What is it?"

He tilted his head and studied her for a moment. "A mistake."

His response didn't surprise her. "You regret it."

"I was young and foolish," he answered.

Though, she couldn't imagine him young and foolish. He was so well put together. At only thirty-six, he owned the best criminal law practice in the area. There was something to be said about that.

"Weren't we all," she murmured. "Can I see it?"

Shit. She just asked her boss to take off his shirt. No wonder he stiffened at her request.

She was going to get her ass fired.

She scrambled for cover. "I... I just love body art. I'm fascinated by it."

He pinned her with a stare. "It's hard to see. Black ink on dark skin doesn't show up well."

Rayne lifted a shoulder. "I can be the judge of that."

Fuck. She was pushing her luck. If he handed her a pink slip tomorrow, she was screwed. She finally landed at a firm where she might be able to make partner. A firm where she *wanted* to make partner, one she was proud to be part of. But, her raging hormones were going to screw that all up.

She needed to keep her mouth and her legs shut. When his fingers ripped the loosened tie from his neck and began to slip the buttons out of their holes, she found herself melting into a puddle.

He was actually removing his shirt.

Holy hell.

When he got down to the buttons at his waist, he stood up abruptly, his rolling chair slamming the wall behind him. He tugged the shirt tails out of his pants and finished removing it.

All the while, his eyes never left hers.

Rayne froze in place, like a deer stuck in headlights. She never expected him to take off his shirt. She didn't know what to do. She usually wasn't at a loss for words or actions.

But, it seemed so inappropriate.

And she fucking loved it.

He stood for a moment in his undershirt and suit pants, studying her. "Are you sure?" he finally asked.

The deep-timbre of his voice made her quiver and her nipples pebble painfully. She nodded her head and said with a shaky voice, "Yes."

He ripped his undershirt over his head and tossed it on the desk. In the soft glow from his desk lamp, she ran her gaze over his body. He was thick with muscle, his skin so dark that he was right, it was hard to clearly see the tattoo. As she stepped closer, she could tell it was a dragon. A very large dragon. This was no youthful impulse tattoo. This one took thought, planning. Multiple sittings. The tail ended just past his right elbow, the rest of its length wrapped around his arm, the body of the beast came over his shoulder and down his back, the head resting over his left shoulder. It appeared he carried the weight of the dragon across his shoulders. She wondered what it signified.

As she lightly ran her fingers over his skin, following the pointy spine of the reptile, she wanted to see it in full light.

She wondered how many people knew he had it.

Standing close behind him, she studied the markings, then traced her fingertips up his neck and over his tightly trimmed hair, then around the curves of his ears. He shuddered beneath her touch.

"Have you seen enough?" The question sounded strained.

"No," she whispered. And she hadn't.

"Rayne," came the low warning.

"Boss."

He spun on her and grabbed her shoulders, giving her a little shake. "I told you not to call me that." Then he kissed her.

No, he didn't kiss her. He crushed his lips against her mouth like he owned it. He forced his tongue between her lips and took complete control. His fingers gripped her chin tightly, while his other hand snaked between them to jerk at his belt, rip open his pants, and yank his zipper down.

She struggled for breath as she blindly reached for him, finding his erection, long, hard, thick, and she squeezed. His groan filled her mouth and he struggled to pull her skirt up, but it was too tight to rise high enough to give him access.

With a frustrated growl, he tore away from her and spun her around, unzipping her skirt and pushing it down her hips until it fell around her feet. With a hand to the back of her head, he bent her over and she caught herself by grabbing onto his desk chair. She jerked when he tore a hole in her stockings and yanked her panties aside.

Before she could prepare herself, he pushed inside her with a grunt. He wasn't gentle, there were no soothing words. This was not, in any way, romantic. This was raw fucking. He grabbed her hips and gave it to her as hard and as fast as he could.

With a cry, she closed her eyes as he filled her, stretched her. She'd wanted him from the moment she saw him. But, never expected it to happen, and certainly not like this. Though her fantasies had been close.

His fingers dug into the flesh at her hips and their skin slapped together. Her body tried to accommodate him, but she never expected his size. She tried to relax and open herself up to him, but being in this position didn't help.

But, fuck, when he reached around and jammed his hand down the front of her panties to find her clit, she bit her bottom lip as her inner walls clenched around him, squeezing.

His fast and furious thrusting brought her quickly to the edge.

His thumb pressed and circled her sensitive nub until she couldn't take anymore. *No more.*

As she screamed and her body rippled around him, he released her hip to grab her hair, yanking her head back as he bottomed out one more time, spilling into her. His cock pulsated deep inside her, making her squirm for more. But, he was done. Spent.

Suddenly he stiffened, released her hair, slipped his hand out of her panties, and then slid out of her completely. She didn't move for a moment and only heard his breathing. Fast, heavy, uneven. Then, a curse ripped from him and he stepped back.

Rayne straightened and tugged her skirt up from around her ankles and over her torn stockings, zipping it closed. She didn't turn yet because she didn't know what to expect from him. What to say.

The curse had sounded angry. Full of regret.

Though, she had none of her own.

She'd gotten what she'd wanted. Maybe not how she'd hoped. But—

Then reality hit her like a splash of cold water and a chill went through her.

Still facing the windows, she said, "Oh my God. I need this job. Please. This never happened."

He stood only inches away, but it felt like a mile on a cold winter's day. "Right. This never happened," he repeated in a flat tone from behind her.

She glanced up, met his eyes in the reflection of the glass, then pushed past him in a rush to escape his office.

He had no right to call Holloway irresponsible. What he did with Rayne was just as bad.

No condom. An employee. In his office, no less.

He'd been avoiding her for the past couple of weeks. Keeping his office door closed, coming in early, leaving late. Anything to keep from facing her. From facing the reality of his own loss of control.

Hell, anything to keep from bending her over and fucking her again and again.

Her normal habit of "popping into his office" had stopped since that night. He figured she regretted their actions as much as he did.

He had to man up and stop avoiding her. As her boss, he should be her mentor.

What a fine one he turned out to be.

So today, he kept his door open like normal hoping to catch a peek of her as she walked by in those sexy high heels of hers. Or, hoping she'd pop her head in, acting like nothing happened and things were back to normal.

Gryff blew out a noisy breath. *Normal. Right.*

A ruckus sounded from down the hallway, passed his door, and headed in the direction of Rayne's office. He thought he caught a glimpse of tanned skin and dark blond shaggy hair.

He stared at his computer screen and saw nothing. He read the same line of the email over and over, none of it sinking in.

He'd lost his damn mind.

Unable to resist anymore, he called out to Dani. "Did I hear Holloway out there?

"Yes! He has an appointment with Rayne."

Gryff frowned at the excitement in his secretary's voice. *What the fuck.* Did Trey have this effect on all women?

He closed his eyes and clenched his fingers into fists, fighting the urge to rush down the hall to interrupt them, make sure they weren't being inappropriate, being too friendly.

Touching.

He sat there for two more beats before pushing to his feet. "Hold my calls," Gryff called over his shoulder to Dani as he strode past her and down the hallway, not even skipping a beat.

With legs wide and fists pinned to his side, he stood staring at

Rayne's closed office door. Then he heard noises, voices, and he shoved the door open, the blood rushing in his ears.

Trey's hands gripped her shoulders as he stood behind her, leaning over, his face almost pressed to hers. He spoke low into her ear.

Her eyes were bright, her face flushed.

Gryff couldn't miss her hard nipples pressing against her tight, satin blouse. As he watched her lips part and her pink tongue sweep across the bottom one, he felt a painful squeeze all the way down to his balls.

Trey didn't bother to straighten, just flashed Gryff a Cheshire cat smile instead.

It took everything Gryff had to not leap over the desk and pound the shit out of him.

Trey must have noticed his murderous look because the twinkle left his eye and he slowly straightened but not before saying something quietly into her ear.

That bothered him, but not as much as what the man said next.

"You said you didn't have dibs."

"And I said to keep your dick out of my best attorney."

Rayne's mouth dropped and her brows furrowed. She shifted forward in her chair to dislodge Trey's hands from her shoulders. "What?"

Her gaze bounced from one to the other, but Gryff ignored her to stare down Trey instead.

Finally, Trey stepped away from her, holding his palms out in surrender.

"He's here to sign his agreement of terms and give me the retainer," Rayne said, her voice tinged with anger. She waved the check at Gryff.

"Five hundred G's as agreed," Trey said, coming around Rayne's desk and patting Gryff on the back. He leaned close, his hand landing on Gryff's ass. "You know you can join us. There's nothing wrong with a good threesome. Ask your brother."

Gryff's nostrils flared and a muscle in his jaw popped. He turned his head only long enough to ask Rayne, "Are you done with your business?"

"Yes."

He turned back to Trey, dislodging his hand. "Then get out."

Gryff was going to kill his brother.

Trey smiled. "You have a great ass, Gryff. I bet the three of us could have a good time together. Think about it."

Before Gryff knew what he was doing, he had Trey pinned to the wall with a forearm pressed against the other man's throat. He shoved his face into Trey's. His breathing came harsh, as did Trey's. They stared each other down for a second. Two.

He ignored the noise coming from the direction of Rayne's desk.

"I don't need to think about it," Gryff growled. "You're not going to fuck either one of us."

Trey's jaw tightened, like he instinctively wanted to fight back, but he didn't. He allowed Gryff to overpower him. Which was smart. Trey might be a professional athlete, but Gryff was bigger, heavier, and stronger than the quarterback. It wouldn't take much to pound the guy into the ground. The four guys he beat up must have been pussies.

"You know how to turn a guy on, Gryff. You gave me a hard-on." Trey's words sounded strained from the pressure on his windpipe.

His words were true; the man's erection pressed against Gryff's thigh.

"Boss."

Gryff blinked but didn't let up.

"Boss, don't. Let him go."

"You know, we can share. It's worth it. Ask your brother."

"Next time you say 'ask your brother' I will rip your fucking tongue out."

Trey chuckled, but it came out more like choking. "If you do that, I won't be able to suck your dick. And I'm good at it, Gryff. Picture it:

me down on my knees, your cock in my mouth, your fingers gripping my hair as I swallow your load."

Gryff grimaced but still didn't back off. However, he couldn't wipe that vision from his mind.

"I know you want it, too, Gryff. I can feel you getting just as hard as me."

Fuck. He was right.

Gryff stepped back abruptly, letting him go. Trey's hand went to his throat.

"Get. Out." It should be fury making his voice shake, but it wasn't. Gryff didn't want to admit what made his fingers tremble and his body react.

With a smirk, Trey gave Rayne a last look before heading out the door. "You have my number, Gryff, if you want me."

Gryff slammed the door behind him and got control of his breathing before spinning to face Rayne.

She no longer had the gleam in her eye or the color in her cheeks. In fact, she looked a little shell-shocked. "Jesus, Boss," she whispered. Her eyes dropped to his groin and his obvious erection.

Fuck.

He didn't know if she was "Jesus, Bossing" him because of his loss of temper or because of his body's reaction to Trey.

Either way it wasn't good, and he wasn't proud of himself. Not at all. He worked long and hard to get where he was in life. And suddenly, his control seemed to be tumbling down around him. First with Rayne. And now Trey.

He strode over to her chair and spun her to face him. He looked down into her face, wanting to watch her expression when he asked, "You want him?"

She didn't even hesitate. "Yes."

He sucked in a breath. "So, once was enough with me?"

Now she hesitates.

"No."

"What does that mean?"

"I want you, Gryff, but not bent over in your office only because you're pushed past the point of no return. I want you so much more than like that."

He gave a sharp nod. More to himself than to her. He snagged her chin in his fingers, tilting her head up so she couldn't avoid his eyes. "You can't have us both. I won't share you with him."

When she said nothing, he realized he was not only jealous of Trey's interest in Rayne, but also of her interest in Trey.

That was just plain fucked up.

"I can take care of that for you," she whispered.

He opened his mouth to ask her what she was talking about. But he knew. Now it wasn't Trey keeping him hard, it was Rayne. His damn cock just wouldn't quit.

He dragged his thumb slowly over her bottom lip, over her bright red lipstick, then dipped it inside. When the tip of her tongue touched him, he locked his knees so he wouldn't fall to her feet. It was a mistake to even consider what she proposed.

But, damn, he couldn't stop. And he couldn't forget what it felt like when he pounded her a couple weeks ago.

Without waiting for his answer, and not breaking eye contact, she unbuckled his belt and opened his pants.

This was wrong. Even if it wasn't so wrong, there wasn't a lock on the door. Which was wrong.

He didn't stop her from pushing his pants and boxer briefs down enough to take him into her palm. Then, she pulled her chin from his grasp and wrapped those red lips around him.

His fingers slipped into her long hair and gripped it tight as his head fell back, his eyes slid shut and his mouth parted to release short breaths. His chest constricted as her wet, hot, sweet, sweet mouth took him deep. With fingers wrapped around the root of his cock, the pull of her mouth made him groan and thrust.

His balls tightened when she scraped her nails over the delicate skin. It was her tongue lapping at the crown of his head then working its way down his length that made him cry out.

He guided her head, that filthy, sexy mouth of hers up and down his length, the muscles in his ass clenching and unclenching as she swallowed him, dipped the tip of her tongue in his slit.

Even though he knew it was Rayne who had him in her mouth, he couldn't erase what Trey told him. The image of Trey down on his knees and it being *his* mouth on him wouldn't disappear.

He forced his eyes open so he could see who held him, who sucked him. Who really turned him on. Not who he imagined it to be.

There was something about her that drove him over the edge way too soon. Maybe it was her sex-kitten looks, the curve of her lips, those bold green eyes. Her sultry smile, her husky voice, her full breasts that seemed to want to spill out of her blouse.

Whatever it was, it took him to his knees. She sucked, licked, and scraped her teeth over the head of his cock, squeezing his balls all the while. Seeing her red lips stretched over his girth, her cheeks hollowed, her eyes catching his, sent any thoughts of Trey spinning away.

When the pressure built and his dick got even harder, he knew he wouldn't last. And hell, right now he wanted this to last forever, but it would end embarrassingly quicker than he'd like. Just like that time he had her bent over. Fast and furious.

And that was all she wrote, folks. He was a complete goner. His chest heaved, his hips jerked and before he could warn her, he released himself at the back of her throat, using his grip in her hair to hold her still.

A few seconds later his fingers finally loosened and he freed her. "Sorry."

She straightened in her chair and wiped the corners of her mouth.

Damn, even that was hot.

"For what?"

For thinking of Trey Holloway even for a second while you blew my mind. "For no warning."

"I wouldn't have done anything different even if you had."

Fuuuuuuuuck.

He tucked himself back in his pants and fastened them closed before taking a step back. "This is crazy," he said, shaking his head, scrubbing a palm over his hair.

"Why?"

He leveled his gaze at her in surprise. "Why? Because I'm your boss. This is my place of business. And this is not very professional."

And, let's not forget the part where you're destroying my control.

Not good.

And on that note, he needed to get the hell out of there, before he shoved her onto her desk and took advantage of his employee again. He rounded her desk and yanked her office door open. He needed to escape while he still could.

"Boss," she called out. He stopped dead in the doorway, his back to her. "I like you and I think you know what I mean when I say that. But, as bad as this might sound, I like him, too. Is that wrong? I don't know. But there's something about him underneath the surface and it's the same with you. You don't want anyone to know, but I see something. You two seem like complete opposites, even if only on the surface, but that's what attracts me to both of you."

Not as opposite as you think.

"But you can't expect exclusivity. We're not even dating."

And there it was. The truth. They weren't even dating. He didn't even know if he wanted to open that can of worms with an employee.

It wasn't smart.

But then neither was fucking her in his office or her sucking him off in hers.

He could fire her...

What the fuck.

Was he stupid enough to fire one of his best attorneys just to get a piece of tail?

His brain was truly scrambled. Especially if he thought Rayne was just a piece of tail. Because there was so much more to her than that.

He couldn't answer her, so he only nodded and closed her office door quietly behind him.

Then spent the rest of the day holed up in his office, reminding himself why he got that dragon tattoo in the first place.

CHAPTER 3

T rey knew this might be a bad idea.

A really bad one.

But, he figured it could be worth the risk. Though, last time he was in a bar thinking he would get lucky, he got arrested and then suspended from the team, instead.

And now he was down five hundred grand.

Five. Hundred. Fucking. Grand.

He figured he had two good reasons to cough up that much scratch. One, his career might come to a screeching halt if he didn't, and two, he needed to hire the best to represent him, who, with any luck, would get his charges dismissed instead of going through a lengthy legal process. Because if they weren't, it would delay him getting back on the team. And a loss of possibly getting a Super Bowl ring.

He fucking wanted that ring. He could taste it.

Grae Ward said his brother was the best. However, Trey didn't fork out those ridiculous funds simply because of Gryff and Rayne's reputation. Though, once he met both of them he knew he wanted no one else.

He wasn't just talking representation in a court of law. He was talking about his bed. Though, he couldn't figure out who he wanted more. The hot male attorney with an ass that wouldn't quit. Or the hot female attorney with an ass that wouldn't quit.

So, what the hell, why not both? Right?

Right. Though, Gryff probably wouldn't cooperate with his little plan, even though the man got turned on when Trey "flirted" with him. That reaction left Trey with no doubt that Gryff wasn't completely against the idea of being with another man. Whether that stubborn guy wanted to admit it or not.

Yeah, there was no mistaking the hard-on Gryff got when he pinned Trey against the wall.

Now, as he sat at the bar surrounded by stale smoke and after-work drinking habits, he questioned his idea of tricking Gryff here to the bar.

He ran a finger down the sweating glass of his Jack and Coke. The one he had only two sips from.

Because he needed to be sober for this.

He'd be a fool otherwise. Plus, he needed to keep his "nose clean" or he'd watch his five hundred G's go up in smoke. *Poof.*

The door opened and some fresh air rushed into the dank bar's interior, reminding the occupants for a split second that there really *was* a life outside this drinking hole. He had picked this particular place because he hoped no one would recognize him, and if they did, they'd likely leave him alone.

When he first walked in and moseyed up to the bar, eyes had landed on him. Along with looks of recognition and curiosity, he even scored a few chin lifts from some of what looked like regulars. But, so far, no one had violated his personal space.

Even the bartender had left him alone after serving him.

Trey's eyes tracked the broad, dark man approaching him.

And the guy didn't look happy. Not pleased at all.

Though, that was to be expected. Gryffin Ward, Esquire extraordinaire, probably thought himself too good to hang out in bars. He probably thought he had a reputation to uphold. He wouldn't want to risk even a slight smudge on his character by being caught in a place like this. With a guy like him.

Trey grew up in these types of bars. Especially since his drunk of a mother couldn't afford a babysitter for him and his younger sister due to drinking all her money. Which had never been much to begin with.

He had come from shit. So, anything other than shit was an improvement.

"Let's go," came the low demand as Gryff approached him.

"Hold on."

"No. You called me because you said you had too much to drink and couldn't drive. Which, if I remember correctly, I told you no drinking. I guess you thought I was bullshitting. Then you have the fucking balls to call me to come pick your ass up. And, fucking fool that I am, I came. So here I am. Now, let's fucking go."

Damn. Someone crawled out of the wrong side of bed this morning. "Gryff—"

"No, Trey. I'm warning you. I could buy a really nice fucking boat with five hundred thousand. A *really* nice boat. One you'll never step foot on. Just remember that. And remember that when that Super Bowl ring slides on someone else's finger."

Trey frowned and stared up into the angry mask of the other man's face. "Well, that was just downright cold."

"You're damn right it was. I'm simply reminding you of what you have to lose. And let me tell you what you have to gain if you fuck up... jail time. Since you like men, it may not be such a hardship for you. But you won't get to pick your partners. Though, maybe you're not picky and any dick will do."

Trey closed his eyes and murmured, "Fuck you."

"Look at me, Trey. Now."

Trey's gaze climbed the man standing over him. Gryff shoved a finger in his face. "I don't need irresponsible, cocky assholes like you for clients. I only took you on as a favor for my brother. I really don't need the hassle, let me remind you of that. I wasn't kidding when I said to keep your nose clean. You make our job harder when you don't. So, I want to know why you called me, of all people, to come get your ass because you're drunk."

Fuck. This was not going as planned. Not at all. "I'm not."

Gryff dropped his hand and some of the hardness slipped from his face. "Not what?"

"Not drunk."

Gryff's eyes dropped to the drink in front of him. He turned his head toward the bartender who stood at the farthest end of the bar, watching them from a safe distance. He called out, "How many drinks has he had?"

The bartender lifted one finger. "That's his first."

Gryff frowned as he studied the full drink for another second then leveled his gaze at Trey. "Then why am I here?"

"When's the last time you've tied on a good one?"

Gryff pinned him with a stare, his brows dropping even lower. "Are you serious right now? Please tell me you're not being serious."

"I'll buy you a drink if you come sit with me. I want to make peace. I want things to be smooth between us."

"Smooth," Gryff repeated like he had a bad taste in his mouth.

Trey called down the bar, "Bartender, can you get him whatever he wants?"

The bartender scuttled to them and gave Gryff a questioning look.

"What I want is for you to keep your shit clean," he said in a low voice, but then turned to the bartender and said, "Whatever he's having."

Trey smothered his smile. Baby steps. That's all it took. Baby steps. A few uncomfortable moments later, the bartender slid a glass in front of Gryff. Trey pushed to his feet, grabbed both of their drinks and tilted his head toward one of the empty booths.

"C'mon. Sit with me." Trey leaned close, but didn't touch him. "I won't bite. I promise. Not unless you ask me to."

Gryff shook his head and moved toward a booth farthest from

the other patrons. Trey followed, still fighting the smile that wanted to break out.

When the other man slid into one side, Trey slid into the other, placing Gryff's Jack and Coke in front of him. Without hesitation, Gryff picked it up and downed half of it.

Trey looked at him in surprise.

"You're driving me to drink," was the gruff answer he got in response.

Trey didn't fight the laugh, and he lifted his own glass to his lips, letting the cool drink slide down his throat and warm his stomach. Though, he didn't need help in that area since the man sitting across from him did that all on his own.

Gryffin Ward was fucking hot as hell. Trey was almost as determined to get him in his bed as a Championship ring on his finger.

But baby steps, he reminded himself. He didn't feel like getting his block knocked off. Trey was certain that getting his ass beat by Gryff would be worse than the four guys who tried to take him down the last time.

"I really respect your brother."

Gryff swallowed the rest of his drink, slammed the glass on the table, then eyed him suspiciously. "Me, too."

Trey raised a hand to the bartender. "Keep 'em coming." Then turned back to face him. "You guys look a lot alike."

Gryff simply said, "We're blood."

"Are you alike in any other ways?"

The bartender came up, placed a fresh drink in front of Gryff and disappeared. He stared at it before saying, "Look, you call me up to take your drunk ass home. It turns out you lied and now you want to get *me* drunk, so what gives?" Then he pinned his dark eyes on Trey. "Are you trying to booze me up enough to get me out behind the bar for a make-out session?" When Trey didn't answer, he continued, "You want to lure me back there so you can get your ass kicked again?"

"I didn't get my ass kicked."

"No, you busted up a few guys instead. You should be proud of yourself."

The man didn't give an inch. He was hard, relentless. And once again, Trey realized his plan to soften up Gryff was backfiring. "Fuck you, Gryff. I protected myself."

"And you got arrested doing it."

"What was I supposed to do? Let them beat the shit out of me? Kill me? All because I like men? That fucker did, too. He just didn't want anyone to know and had to save face when he got caught red-handed with his tongue down my throat."

"Here's a thought... Maybe don't pick up random men in bars. Or stick to women."

Trey snorted and dragged his fingers through his hair. "Right."

"Why not?"

"Because I want what I want."

"We don't always get what we want. It's part of being grown."

"No, Gryff, you're wrong. Being grown means you work hard until you achieve your goal."

"When have you ever worked hard? You were handed a dream spot on a professional football team. You make millions to throw a damn ball."

"You don't think being a professional athlete is hard work? You think I didn't work for it? Ask your fucking brother how hard I worked to become a first-round draft pick. They courted me because I'm that good."

"Then don't fuck it up," came the soft reply. Gryff's finger circled the rim of his glass.

Trey's anger quickly dissipated as he studied the man across from him. His second drink was half gone already. Maybe the man did know how to loosen up. That gave him some hope.

"I'm not trying to fuck it up," he murmured, then took another sip of his own drink. He waved at the bartender to bring them another round.

Gryff sighed. "I'm here to drive you home. Plying me with drinks won't be conducive to that."

"I've got it covered, don't worry. Just relax and make peace with me."

"Speaking of peace," Gryff finished the rest of his second drink in one swallow. "You want a piece of me?"

The direct question surprised Trey. "Is the truth going to make you uncomfortable?"

"Probably."

"I think you already know the truth. I haven't hidden my interest the couple times we were face to face at your office." Or dick to dick. But he'd keep that one to himself.

"Why me?"

"Have you seen your ass?"

Gryff frowned and took the glass directly from the bartender as he approached the booth. He downed half of it before placing it on the table. "But you want Rayne, too?"

"Have you seen *her* ass?" Trey chuckled when Gryff's eyes crinkled and the corners of his lips twitched.

"She drives me nuts," Gryff grumbled.

"How so?"

Gryff hesitated a few beats before asking, "Have you seen her ass?"

Trey's howl of laughter filled their corner of the bar and he slammed his hand on the table. "Holy shit, dude." The door opened again and the subject of their conversation headed toward them. Trey leaned forward and whispered, "Speaking of... Here she comes."

Gryff's eyes widened, and he glanced over his shoulder. "What the fuck. Why is she here?"

"I called her right after I called you."

"Why did you call her?"

"Because we're both going to need a ride after we get shit-faced."

Before Rayne made it halfway across the bar, Trey had a hard-on. She wore a green wrap-around dress that was tight and short and matched those emerald green eyes of hers. The V neck of the dress did nothing to hide her cleavage. She wore strappy heels that had a ribbon or something of that nature winding up around her calves. Trey suddenly found it difficult to swallow.

As much as Trey liked men, he had to admit this woman did it for him. She was the complete package: Intelligent, beautiful, successful. Basically, hell on heels. He had done some research and Gryff was right, she was good at what she did. Very good. She might look like luscious eye candy on the outside, but inside this woman was a brilliant diamond. She knew her shit, no doubt about it.

She gave them a breathy, "Hey," when she stopped at the end of the table. And when she smiled, the bar suddenly wasn't so dank anymore.

"Hey," Trey answered, fighting not to touch his cock. "Want a drink?"

She shook her head, her mane of reddish-blonde hair sweeping around her shoulders. He wanted to shove his face in it and take a great big inhale then rub that silkiness all over his body.

"No. I thought I'm the designated driver. Isn't that why you called me?"

"Yep," he answered, giving her a grin, then slid over to give her room to sit next to him.

She eyeballed him for a moment, shot Gryff a look, then slipped in the booth beside him. When her thigh brushed his, his cock jerked in his jeans. *Goddamn.* He wanted those thighs wrapped around his ears.

"So, what's the occasion?" she asked, pinning her boss with a stare.

"Occasion?" Gryff asked her.

"Yes, why you two are suddenly chummy and out drinking together," she explained, not taking her eyes off him.

"I was tricked."

Her brows lifted. "Ah."

"And you were, too," Gryff finished.

Her eyebrows dropped. "Oh."

Ah, shit. Trey needed to save face. "I only had the best intentions, though. Seriously."

"Right," Gryff mumbled into his drink and this time it was him who waved at the bartender for another one. He put up two fingers.

Trey continued, "Well, if anyone knows how important it is for a team to work well together, it's me. And we're now a team, right?"

Gryff leaned back in the booth, angling his long legs out. He crossed his ankles and then his arms over his chest, stared at Trey for a moment before giving Rayne a look. "You believe his bullshit?"

Rayne bit her bottom lip, glanced at the table and laughed. "Sure."

Gryff half-smiled and said, "Then at least one of us does."

"Teams need to be a well-oiled machine," Trey added.

"Oh, Christ," Gryff said, shaking his head and rolling his eyes. "Just stop while you're ahead."

Gryff sat up straight and leaned across the table towards Rayne. "You want to know the real reason he tricked us here?"

Oh shit.

Rayne shrugged and didn't even bother to ask why because Gryff was on a roll.

"Because he wants to fuck you." Gryff paused and raised a finger. "And that's not all. He wants to fuck me. Or me to fuck him. Whatever."

Rayne blinked, then smiled at Gryff. "Yes, I know." She shrugged again. "He hasn't hidden his intentions from the beginning."

Gryff slammed his shoulders against the back of the booth and blew out a breath. He rubbed both hands over his face, then looked at Rayne. "Oh, Jesus. Am I the only one resisting here?"

"Yes," Trey and Rayne both said simultaneously.

Gryff's faced closed up and his eyes narrowed. "Wait. Have you two..." He wagged a finger between the two of them.

"No," they said in sync once more.

Trey watched relief cross Gryff's face. The man was definitely territorial over Rayne for some reason. "You said you didn't have dibs," he said slowly. "Am I missing something?"

Trey's gaze bounced between the two of them. Both of their faces went blank. That was all the answer he needed. He wasn't sure what to think about that little tidbit. It could either help or hinder his intentions. "I think I need another drink."

"Me, too. Bartender!" Gryff called out. "Another round."

CHAPTER 4

Rayne's eyes slid sideways to the man in her passenger seat. No doubt he was feeling good. She then peeked in her rearview mirror. And so was the one in the back.

The later the evening became, the looser the men became. Not that Trey needed any help, but Gryff? Yeah, he needed the booze to get the stick out of his ass and contemplate Trey's suggestion of the three of them hooking up.

Amazingly enough, Trey had talked them into going back to his place. It surprised her when Gryff agreed. Still, she had no idea where things would go from there.

But whatever happened tonight, she was all in. How could she not be? Two handsome, hot, successful men. Anyone in their right mind wouldn't say no. Of course not.

The only issue looming? Gryff was her boss and Trey her client. That may be not only an issue, but a *big* one. And possibly the fact that she was the only one a hundred percent sober. Not that either of the men were sloppy or falling down drunk, but they both seemed loose and happy. Besides, it was nice to see Gryff like that. The more he smiled and laughed, the more Rayne couldn't help but fall for him.

Which, again, reminded her of the not-so-small matter of him being her boss. *Damn.*

He didn't stick his dick in company ink.

No, that wasn't right.

He didn't stick his pen in company pussy.

Nope. Not right either.

Well, either way, it was too late. His cock had been inside her and they both had liked it. *Really* liked it. Once wasn't enough for her. And from what she could tell, not enough for him either.

She pulled her SUV into a secured lower level parking garage after Trey waved a keycard at the card reader. As he directed her to one of his reserved spots, she couldn't help but notice the rows of high dollar vehicles. Seemed as though no one who lived here drove a Honda or a Ford. She almost felt like she was slumming it in her Lexus. She pulled in next to a blacked-out Maserati GranTurismo convertible.

"You've got to be kidding me," Gryff said, staring at the car next to them. "Don't tell me that's yours."

"Then I won't tell you," came the serious answer from the backseat.

"You fucking athletes don't know how to spend your money wisely."

"Hey, it was cheaper than a Bentley."

Gryff snorted, pushed open his door, and unfolded his large frame out of the car. He leaned back in before saying, "It better give a hell of a blow job." Then slammed the door shut.

Rayne hesitated and turned to study Trey. "I hope you know what you're doing."

"Are you asking if I have a plan to tame the beast?"

"Something like that."

"I'm just going to wing it."

She sighed. "Can you at least give me directions to the nearest hospital? Just in case I need to take your bloody pulp there in a hurry."

Trey shook his head and laughed before climbing out of the car. She hurried to follow him since someone with a sound mind needed to be the referee if anything got out of hand.

"I sure hope you think it'll be worth the trouble," she whispered to him as she watched Gryff walk around the convertible, checking it out and mumbling.

"You tell me, is he worth it?"

She frowned.

Trey stroked his hand down her bare arm and she shivered at his electric touch. "Relax, Rayne. Baby steps." He wandered away to join Gryff.

Baby steps? What did he mean by that?

She studied the two men practically jerking off over a piece of machinery. What was she getting herself into? What was she getting Gryff into?

She sighed and joined them.

Minutes later they were up in the penthouse of the high-rise building. Trey actually needed to use his keycard to get the elevator to rise to his floor. And for good reason. As the doors swooshed open, it led directly into his—what he called—"apartment." Rayne had never been in an "apartment" like this. It comprised half the top floor. Even half the top floor was nothing to sneeze at.

"I hope you have a financial advisor," was all that Gryff said as he stepped into Trey's world.

"This was an investment. I own it," Trey announced, sounding proud of himself.

"Well, bully for you," Gryff answered as he wandered over to the expanse of windows overlooking the city. The view was spectacular, the city lights beautiful in the dark of night.

"And guess who my next-door neighbor is?" Trey asked as he moved to the middle of his expansive living room.

When Gryff ignored him, he looked to Rayne and wiggled his eyebrows, so she felt obligated to ask, "Who?"

"Cole Dixon."

Gryff froze, then turned to Trey. "I bet you and he hooked up a time or two."

"Why do you think that? Just because neither of us have any sexual hang-ups?"

"Who's Cole Dixon?" Rayne asked finally. She was lost.

Trey's mouth dropped. "You don't know who Dix is?"

"If she knew she wouldn't ask," Gryff growled. Sounded like her boss was getting cranky again.

"No, no idea," she said and moved closer to Gryff, tempted to rub his arm to soothe him. She just wasn't sure if it was a good idea to pet her boss. Though, she did suck his dick a couple days ago.

Jesus. She mentally shook her head to clear her debauched thoughts.

"Dix is only *the* best running back in Bulldogs' history and lover to Lawrence "Long Arm" Landis, who was *the* best quarterback in Bulldogs' history. I plan on following in Ren's footsteps and bringing us home the Championship trophy."

"*If* you can get back on the team."

"*When* I get back on the team."

Gryff made a noise and stepped closer to the windows, staring out.

"So, they live on the other side?" Rayne asked.

"They actually live on the beach with their wife Eve and their new kid. They only use the place when they come into the city."

"Wait. They have a wife and kid?"

"Yeah. They all hooked up and then got knocked up."

She bet that was an interesting dynamic. However, she thought she heard a rumor at the office about Gryff's older brother doing something similar. Couldn't be.

Rayne's brows pinned together. "Let me get this straight—"

"It's just like Gryff's brother. He hooked up with a married couple and they all live together now. I don't think there's any buns in the oven yet, though. Is there, G?"

"Don't call me G," Gryff said to the window.

"Call him Boss, he really likes that," Rayne suggested with a helpful smile.

"Rayne," came the low warning.

"Yeah. *Boss*. I like that," Trey went on, missing the displeasure in Gryff's voice.

Gryff finally spun around. "You call me Boss and you might find yourself flapping your arms to see if you can fly when I toss you from the balcony."

Rayne pinned her lips together to keep from laughing.

He scowled at her. "Rayne, don't encourage him."

"Yes, Boss," she said.

He bowed his head and shook it, his hands planted on his hips. "I think I need more booze."

"Sorry, I suck as a host. I'll get you a drink," Trey said and then disappeared.

Rayne moved closer to Gryff and met his eyes. "Your brother is in a threesome?"

"Yes."

"With a married couple?"

"Yes."

"And it works?"

Gryff nodded his head slightly. "It works."

"Damn," she whispered in awe.

"That's what I thought. But it works well, actually."

She stared at his full lips, the color of a ripe Bing cherry. "Huh."

"Are you getting ideas?"

She knew exactly where she wanted those lips. "I already had them."

"You said you wanted both of us."

She hesitated. She wanted what she wanted and there was no point in lying about it. Skirting the truth would get her nowhere. "Yes, but I didn't think you'd go for both at the same time."

"I didn't say I would." He snagged her chin and tilted her face up so she couldn't avoid his eyes. "I alone wouldn't be enough for you."

"I didn't say that," she whispered, then licked her lips, his eyes following the movement of her tongue. A jolt shot through her, landing in her core, making her warm and wet between her thighs.

"But you want Trey, too."

"Yes. I told you that."

"You certainly did."

Time to go for broke... "Are you willing?"

His expression closed up and his eyes narrowed before he asked, "To watch another man fuck you?"

"To participate." Her lips parted, and the breath rushed out of her at the thought of the three of them together.

"In a threesome? With another man? I don't know."

"I know you're attracted to him. I saw your reaction the other day in my office."

Something flashed in his eyes before he hid it. "A fluke."

Rayne smiled softly but shook her head, dislodging his grip on her chin. "No. I don't think so."

Gryff lifted a shoulder. "Think what you'd like."

Rayne placed a hand on his chest and slid it down to his stomach. His muscles shifted beneath her fingers. "Boss—"

"Every time you call me that it gives me a hard-on."

Her lips curved into a smile. "I know."

Gryff curled a strand of her hair around his finger and studied it. "I want to fuck you tonight."

"Yes, I want that, too."

"But, here we are standing in the middle of Trey Holloway's living room instead. You could be in my bed right now, that green dress on my floor, your legs over my shoulders."

"Or, we can head to Trey's bed and have him join us."

His head tilted and his eyes raked her face. "Why do you want this?"

She answered, "Why not?" Because she really had no answer to give him. Other than she was being greedy by wanting two men in her bed at once. "Have you ever thought about it?"

"Maybe with two women. Isn't that every heterosexual man's fantasy? But not with another man, no."

"If you don't touch?"

"Have two men over six-feet tall fuck one woman and not touch? Impossible."

"We can take turns," Trey suggested as he closed in on them, carrying drinks in his hands. He offered one to Gryff, who took it, and the other to Rayne. "Just soda," he assured her. He turned back to Gryff. "I can watch you two."

"No."

"You can watch us," Trey suggested, indicating him and Rayne.

"No."

"She can watch the two of us."

"I would love to watch the two of you. Two men together turn me on," Rayne confessed. The thought of the two of them in bed together pooled heat between her legs. She pressed herself against Gryff's hip, her hand still flat against his lower stomach.

Gryff looked down into her face. "Sorry. Not going to happen."

"Then why did you agree to come back to my place?" Trey asked him.

Without breaking eye contact with Rayne, he answered, "I don't know."

"I think you do," Rayne whispered, then added, "*Boss*." She moved her hand over his belt and down to his groin, confirming what she already knew. "Please kiss me, Boss."

"Rayne," he groaned, shoving his drink toward Trey, who scrambled to grab it. He dug his hands into her hair and leaned down to crush his lips to hers. She gasped at the ferocity of it, how he owned her mouth, took control of her tongue. She moaned into his mouth as his fingers clenched into fists, pulling her hair harder.

Finally, he broke the kiss, only pulling away slightly, panting as much as she was.

"Don't stop on my account."

Gryff's eyes closed for a moment, and when they opened, Rayne felt disappointment at the sudden loss when he stepped back. She could see his control physically shutting him down.

"My turn?" Trey asked, slipping in between them, grabbing her shoulders and pulling her against him. His erection was as unmistakable as Gryff's as it pushed against her belly when he lowered his lips to hers. "I've been patiently waiting to do this," he murmured against her before stroking his tongue over her lips, separating them, then dipping inside.

His kiss differed from Gryff's but made her melt against him just the same. He wrapped an arm around her back to pull her tight against his hips, making sure she felt all of him. His other hand went from her hip, up her belly, then cupped her breast over her dress. He pulled away just enough to say, "I want to see you naked."

She wanted to say the same to him, but he took her mouth again, exploring, playing, teasing. She groaned, her nipples hard as he played with them over her dress. When he nipped her lower lip, she gasped, grabbing handfuls of his shirt to keep herself on her feet. Her legs trembled, her pussy throbbed, her arousal made her slick with need.

When Trey finally broke the kiss, she couldn't focus for a second because her head spun. The man could kiss. No doubt about it.

"Your lips are swollen from both our kisses," Trey murmured, not taking his eyes off her face. "They're beautiful."

She smiled and stepped back, reluctantly releasing his shirt. Though she wanted to tear it right off of him.

She peeked around his shoulder, looking for Gryff. He once again stood at the windows, staring out, his back to them, his body stiff. Though from the reflection, she could see his eyes on them.

Watching everything.

"Boss..."

"Fuck, Rayne," he said softly, dropping his head and shaking it.

Rayne fought the panic as Trey approached, stepping close behind him. Almost touching, but not. Gryff lifted his head, but didn't say a word. Trey cautiously ran a hand over Gryff's wide shoulders, almost as if tempting fate by trying to pet a tiger in the wild.

He could lose a limb.

"Fuck you, Trey," Gryff growled, spinning around, grabbing Trey by the throat.

Rayne gasped, and as she lurched forward to get between them, she caught herself and stopped as Gryff kissed Trey just as hard as he'd kissed her. Rayne's mind spun at what she witnessed. Trey made no sudden moves, and Gryff controlled the kiss, pushing Trey backward farther into the room, still directing him by the throat and Gryff's hips bumped the other man's. With each shove, Trey fell back another step until he couldn't help but grab Gryff to catch his balance.

Rayne stood helpless, not knowing what to do in what seemed like more of a power struggle than passion. Trey was allowing Gryff to have the upper hand. For now.

But then Trey stumbled and fell to his knees, breaking their contact, but only for a moment. Gryff quickly opened his belt and his pants, while Trey helped to shove them down to expose his thick, hard length. When Trey wrapped his mouth around him, Gryff closed his eyes, the muscles in his neck bulging, his fingers clenched into fists at his side, a grimace on his face.

Then he opened them, glanced down at Trey and whispered, "Fuck you," before meeting Rayne's wide eyes. She felt silly frozen in place in the middle of the room, watching the two men before her. She almost felt like she intruded on their intimacy, but... not.

Rayne wanted to join them, but she didn't want to disrupt them, either. She wanted the chips to fall where they may between the two. This could bring them closer together or push them apart once it was over. That would be up to Gryff. To Trey. Not her.

However, watching them together drove her desire off the charts. Her panties became soaked, her thighs trembled and her knees wobbled. She couldn't keep standing there like a deer in the headlights of an oncoming car.

She sank onto the leather couch, wiggling her panties down and the hem of her dress up. Once her panties dropped to her ankles, she kicked them off over her heels and spread her thighs. Gryff watched her every move, pinning her with his dark stare. As Trey's head rose and fell at Gryff's groin, she slipped her hand between her legs, spread herself wide so he could see everything, then dragged her fingers between her slick folds. She plunged her other hand into the neckline of her dress, finding her hard, aching nipple and twisted it at the same time she slipped two fingers inside of herself.

Her hips shot off the couch as she came instantly. She bit her lip to stop her cry, but she couldn't control it. Her inner muscles clenched around her fingers, though she wasn't done. Not yet. She wasn't done until Gryff and Trey were.

She released her breast and dropped her hand between her legs, circling her clit in a frenzy while she plunged her fingers in and out, wishing one of them fucked her, instead.

Gryff's fingers found purchase in Trey's hair as he fucked the other man's mouth, his hips matching Trey's rhythm. When Gryff gritted his teeth, Rayne knew he was close to losing it. And, once again, so was she. As she watched the two men, she realized she'd never been so turned on, and as Gryff's hips bucked, so did hers. Then she came at the same time Gryff did, her pussy pulsating around her fingers, drenching them.

She dropped her head back against the couch and closed her eyes as the last of the orgasm faded away, sapping her of her strength.

Then hands were on her, spreading her thighs even wider. Trey, still on his knees, settled this time between *her* legs. He dropped his head, whispering, "I want to taste you," before his mouth found her center, licked along her folds, his tongue flicking her sensitive clit.

Hands dug into her hair and when her head was yanked back she looked up right into Gryff's dark, hooded eyes. He stood behind the couch, his nostrils flaring, his fingers gripping her painfully. She would not tell him to stop, to let go. No, she wanted him to dominate her, take her past the point of no return.

"Touch me, Boss," she groaned. "Please."

"Untie your dress," he demanded.

With shaky fingers, she tore impatiently at the knot and when she finally got it free, she pulled her dress apart, giving him an unfettered view of Trey's head between her legs and her breasts spilling over the cups of her black lacy bra. Her nipples ached for his touch, his mouth, his teeth, but he didn't release the tight grip on her hair. Instead, he dropped his mouth to her stretched throat and scraped his teeth along her delicate skin, down her chest, and nuzzled between the soft mounds of her breasts.

She tugged her bra down and her breasts up so he could latch onto one of her nipples, sucking one deep into his mouth. The tugging sensation creating a direct line of fire through her body to where Trey's mouth wreaked havoc on her pussy. Her hips bucked against Trey's mouth as he sucked her clit and slid two fingers inside her.

Her heart pounded, the blood rushed in her ears, and her eyes closed as they spun her out of control. She couldn't stop the words that spilled from between her lips, encouraging them, cursing them, whimpering for relief. When Gryff sank his teeth into her soft flesh, her body bowed off the couch, and she came again, her muscles contracting around Trey's fingers. She couldn't take any more, her clit had become too sensitive.

"Stop. Stop. Stop," she whispered until Trey looked up her body at her with a question in his eyes. She tried to catch her breath, but Gryff's tongue still swirled along the hard tips of her nipples. With a last nibble along the outer curve of her breast he straightened and released her hair.

Trey sat back on his heels, met Gryff's gaze over her head, and said, "I want to fuck her."

Silence filled the room as seconds ticked by. Rayne was afraid to look at Gryff's face. Without even seeing it, she knew he struggled with Trey's intention.

"I haven't fucked her yet. You have. I haven't had a release yet tonight. You have."

Rayne wasn't so sure Gryff would take pity on the other man and concede. It wasn't like Gryff and her were dating and he certainly didn't own her. "Yes," was all Rayne said and was rewarded with a large, open smile from Trey.

She could feel the tension in the air.

When Gryff finally spoke, his voice low and raw, he said, "You have to wear a condom."

Trey's lips twitched. "Of course." He dug into his back pocket, pulling out his wallet, and within seconds held one up.

Trey pushed to his feet, throwing the condom and the wallet on the nearby coffee table, then stepped back, his fingers going to his shirt. One by one, he slipped the buttons out of their holes, exposing his broad, muscular chest decorated with tattoos. He threw his shirt to the side, his eyes never leaving Gryff, who still stood behind her. Gryff leaned over to press his mouth against her ear, his breathing slightly ragged when he asked, "Do you like what you see?"

His hands cupped her breasts and his thumbs brushed over the tips of her nipples.

"Yes."

When Trey slipped his belt from the loops in his jeans, Gryff whispered, "Do you want him inside you?"

Rayne had to suck oxygen to be able to answer. "Yes."

Trey worked the top button of his jeans open then slid down the zipper. Gryff murmured against her ear, "Are you wet for him?"

"Fuck yes," she moaned. She reached behind her and grabbed the back of his neck, holding him there. She wanted him to continue to talk dirty to her, to hear the deep-timbre of his voice in her ear, making her nipples pebble even harder and her pussy even wetter.

Trey kicked off his shoes and pulled off his socks before shucking his jeans and when he stood before them in just boxer briefs, Rayne could see the hard line of his cock under the fabric, the dark spot in the cotton where his precum had soaked through. He palmed himself over his underwear still watching the both of them, watching Gryff squeeze and pinch her dusky pink nipples between his dark fingers.

"Do you like me touching you, Rayne?"

"Yes, Boss."

"Do you want me to touch you when he's fucking you?"

She shuddered. "Oh yes. Boss, please."

"*Fuck*, Rayne," he groaned in her ear. "You keep that up and I'll fuck your mouth while he fucks your pussy."

"Boss, I want you inside me, too. I want you—"

"Not tonight."

"But—"

"No. Another night. I'll fuck you long and hard until you can no longer stand up."

"Promise?"

"I promise. Let Trey have tonight."

As the subject in question hooked his fingers in his boxer briefs and shoved them down, both Gryff and Rayne became quiet, motionless, as they took in his hard length, the fullness of his sac. Then, he wrapped his fingers around his girth and stroked himself slowly, from root to tip. Then again.

And once more.

Trey moved closer. "I want you both."

"You get Rayne," Gryff answered from behind her, his tone leaving no room for negotiation. He straightened when Trey approached.

"I'll have you both. Maybe not tonight. But soon."

"We'll see."

Rayne feared Trey would push his luck and Gryff might shut the whole thing down if he kept it up.

"Trey, take me," she begged, trying to get his attention off Gryff.

His eyes flicked to her then back to Gryff. "I will, baby, don't worry. There's nothing I want more right now. Will you at least undress?" He directed the last question at the man behind her.

49

Once again, silence filled the room. Rayne twisted enough to look at Gryff. "Yes, please, Boss, let me undress you."

His gaze dropped to her, and he smiled slowly. "Come do it for me."

She couldn't resist his proposition. If he was willing to get naked in front of Trey, then she'd happily volunteer to undress him. Plus, she hadn't seen him completely naked yet, either. It would be like unwrapping a gift. And she couldn't wait to pull the end of that ribbon.

Trey offered his free hand, and she accepted it as he helped her to her feet. She shrugged out of her open dress and removed her bra, squeezing her breasts as it fell to the floor.

"Shoes on or off?" she asked, bending over, pointing her ass toward Gryff.

"Oh fuck, those shoes need to stay on," Trey moaned.

"Whatever you want," she told him.

"I like the sound of that," Trey murmured, giving his cock another stroke.

She glanced at Gryff who hadn't moved from behind the couch. "Am I coming to you, Boss? Or are you coming to me?"

"Come here," he demanded, his voice causing a shiver to run down her spine.

"Yes, Boss," she answered as she moved around the couch. When he didn't turn, she stepped up and wrapped her arms around him to unbutton his shirt from behind. Trey remained on the other side of the couch, stroking himself as she undid Gryff's shirt and pulled it off his shoulders. Then tugged his undershirt over his head, leaving his torso bare, his dark skin gleaming under the recessed lighting.

Even though Gryff blocked her view of Trey, she knew exactly when he noticed the dragon tattoo. His exclamation of "Holy shit," an obvious giveaway. Then, he said, "I never would have expected that of you."

Gryff stiffened slightly under her fingers, but she quickly worked her hands down to his waist, finding his belt and pants still unfastened from earlier. She slipped her hands inside his boxer briefs to find his hot, hard length and she palmed him, squeezed and ran a thumb about the crown, spreading his precum.

"Kick off your shoes," she murmured against the skin of his back.

"You take them off me."

She smiled against him, gave him a nip, then dropped to his feet, sliding his loafers off and slowly rolling down his dress socks, taking her time to brush her fingers along his calves, ankles, toes. Without rising, she tugged down his pants and boxers as one, exposing his thick, muscular thighs, his strong calves. As he stepped out of his pants, she nibbled, kissed, and licked her way back up his legs, over the globes of his ass, then up his spine. He was tall, about six-two, so even with her heels on she could only reach midway up his back, her tongue tracing along the bottom of the dark dragon.

He shuddered under her touch, his head dipping for a moment, then rising again when he said to Trey, "Take her now, or I will." His words made the warmth rush between her thighs. She was so ready for one, the other... or both.

Trey, who had stood mesmerized while watching the two of them interact, jerked into action. No one had to tell him twice. And he knew if Gryff decided to take Rayne for himself, Trey would be left standing out in the cold with his dick in his own hand.

He certainly wasn't going to miss out on the chance to sink himself deep into all her lusciousness. Even if Gryff didn't join in this time. If he had his way, Gryff would join in soon enough, anyway.

Trey felt the undercurrent of Gryff's attraction to him. The man's brain might be telling him one thing, but his body told him quite another. Trey knew it the moment he stood in the middle of Gryff's office and the man had given him the once over. Gryff just needed to admit his desires, as deeply buried as they might be.

As he walked around the couch to the two of them, the large

dragon that laid along Gryff's shoulders fascinated him. He would have to ask its meaning one day over pillow talk.

Baby steps.

"Feel free to join in at any time. I won't be offended and I like to share," he told Gryff before pulling Rayne away from him by the wrist and over to the end of the couch. "How do you want me?" he asked her.

"Any way you want it," she answered and her husky voice made his balls tighten.

He hoped he could hold off long enough to make her at least come once if not twice. But he'd hit his limit of watching and waiting. The sheen on her inner thighs showed just how ready she was. "You're beautiful, baby. And you'll be even more so when your body pulses around mine. I can't wait to watch you let go while I'm inside you."

"Then hurry," she encouraged him, making him chuckle at her impatience. But he understood it, he certainly did.

Then it hit him how he wanted her. And how to involve Gryff without making him too uncomfortable with the situation.

"Gryff, sit on the couch." Instead of waiting to see if the stubborn man did as requested, he lifted Rayne's long, thick hair up and kissed the back of her neck, making her shiver. "You're so fucking sexy."

"You as well," she whispered over her shoulder. "I need you inside me."

When she rubbed her bare ass against his aching cock, he bit back a whimper. When he checked, he saw Gryff sat on the couch, his heavily built, dark body a sharp contrast to the cream-colored leather couch. He looked like a piece of sculpted art sitting there, his body hard everywhere. His erection protruded from his lap, long and thick. He closed his eyes for a moment at the memory of Gryff's load being shot down the back of this throat. Precum leaked from the head of his cock at a faster pace. If he didn't do something soon, it wouldn't be just precum.

"Bend over the end of the couch, baby. Give your mouth to

Gryff... and anything else he wants. That's it. Just like that, baby. Yes. *Fuck.*"

With Rayne's hips draped over the wide arm of the couch, he had the perfect view of her readiness, her ripeness. Her pussy, slick and pink, was like a Siren's call to him.

He might like men, but he loved women as well. The beauty of what was being offered humbled him. Not only could he see the plump folds of her pussy, he could see that tight rosette, tempting him.

He wanted to shake his head to bring back reality, to wake himself up from this dream. Because there was no way he could be lucky enough to have two such beautiful, sexy specimens in his apartment, on his couch. But when Gryff handed him the condom and their fingers brushed, he knew this was no hallucination.

Yes, as a star quarterback, he could get pussy, or even dick, whenever he wanted. But Rayne was no groupie, Gryff no obsessed fan. These were two people who couldn't care less about his fame and fortune. They were here for Trey, the man, not Trey the football player.

That thought alone made him even harder. When he rolled the condom over his length, his cock jerked at his own touch. He lined the head of his cock along her sex, rubbing it in between the wet folds.

"You want me, baby?"

"Yes," she said, her cheek laying on Gryff's thigh, as the other man stroked her hair, her back, but watched Trey's every movement. "Both of you."

Trey met Gryff's gaze and held it when he answered, "Next time, baby. Promise." He groaned as he slid slowly into her warmth. Her muscles tightened around him, squeezing, making his breath hitch, his heart pound. His fingers dug into her hips as he began the age-old rhythm of fucking her thoroughly. She cried out, but that was quickly smothered by Gryff when he lifted her enough to capture her lips, take her nipples between his fingers and twisting.

The longer he pumped, the harder it was to resist at least touching her tight hole. He slipped a finger between them to gather some of her arousal, then circled the bud. With each circle he pressed harder, until she relaxed enough to let him in. His finger kept the rhythm of his cock, over and over until he heard her curse against Gryff's lips, then drop her head back to his lap, taking the other man into her mouth. Gryff raked fingers through her long tresses, letting her keep her own pace. Within seconds a curse slipped from between his lips, too.

As Trey's hips slapped against Rayne's ass, and as he fucked her with his finger, watching Rayne suck Gryff's cock just about undid him. The only thing he wished for was Gryff to be fucking him as he fucked Rayne.

He had to make that happen. Not tonight, though. For tonight they took baby steps. He would gratefully accept whatever Gryff allowed.

Rayne clenched around him, her back bowed, and she moaned around Gryff's cock. Gryff's eyes shut and his head dropped back for a moment, his fingers now gripping her hair tightly, his hips lifting slightly off the couch. Then his eyes opened, and he turned his head towards Trey, watching him pump in and out of the woman on his lap.

Trey was about to lose it. There was no way he could hold out anymore. But he wanted one thing first...

"C'mere," Trey commanded, hoping he'd listen.

Gryff leaned closer and Trey bent over Rayne's back until their mouths met. Trey pressed his tongue between Gryff's lips until they opened, letting him in. The man's lips were soft and broad, and he couldn't wait to have them wrapped around his cock. At the thought, Trey gasped, breaking the contact. He was about to explode.

"I'm going to fucking come," Gryff moaned, as Rayne's head raised and lowered in his lap.

"Me, too," Trey groaned, reaching under Rayne to find her clit and with one finger pressed in her ass and another rubbing her sensitive nub, the second he felt her tighten around him, he cried out, releasing into her, his cock pulsing as her pussy milked him dry. He stilled, deep inside her, and watched the last few seconds of Gryff's control disappear.

A few moments later, when breathing had slowed and heart rates returned to almost normal, Rayne lifted her head and looked over her shoulder at him, a smile on her face. "When can we do this again?"

CHAPTER 5

Gryff didn't want to admit he was freaked out, but he was fucking freaked out. Just a little bit. Okay, maybe more than that.

As he paced his brother's kitchen, Grae frowned at him, his arms folded across his chest and his ankles crossed as he leaned back against the counter. "Seriously, you need to calm down."

He knew he needed to listen to his brother, but he was unraveling. And for good reason. "I'm scared." Gryff didn't miss the answering raise of eyebrows.

"About what?"

"A *situation*."

"Situation," Grae repeated, shaking his head and chuckling. "You mean a relationship?"

"You laugh, but this type of stuff is easy for you."

His older brother suddenly got serious. "Easy? What part of any relationship is easy?"

"It's easy for you because you've done this before—which I didn't know until our lovely sister let it slip—and you're doing it again. So, you must like it."

Grae shook his head, clearly confused. Gryff wasn't surprised his brother was confused because he was, too.

"First of all, Gryff, this is nothing like the last time. The last time was a disaster. And second, a relationship with one person is hard enough. Try two. Luckily for the most part, Connor is easy-going. Paige? Well, Paige is Paige. Enough said. And how is your *situation* even similar to mine?"

"But you love them."

Grae hesitated. "Yes. But we're not talking about love here, right? Or am I missing something?"

Gryff shook his head and began to pace again, his fingers interlocked behind his neck.

"Brother, talk to me," Grae encouraged, his tone a little softer.

"No. Not love. I mean... Rayne... She's so fucking... I don't know... Irresistible. From the moment I met her, the second she sat across from me in her interview. Hell, the morning of her first day at the firm. And definitely the first time she burst into my office calling me Boss." Gryff blew out a breath at the memory.

"Boss?"

"Yeah, she calls me that all the time." Gryff added quickly, "I don't like it."

"So, tell her to stop."

"I did."

"And?"

He shrugged as he paced past Grae for the umpteenth time. "Like Paige, Rayne is Rayne. And she likes to call me that."

"And you think you don't like it because you shouldn't, but you actually do."

"*Fuck.*" Gryff stopped dead in his tracks and reluctantly admitted, "It turns me on."

Silence greeted him and he spun on his heels to face Grae. Finally, his brother said, "Ah."

Ah? Yeah, fuck, like that helped a whole lot.

"But there's nothing between you two besides just wanting to pump her full of your cum, right?"

Gryff's jaw hit the floor. He collected it and slapped it back into place. "What the hell happened to my uptight brother?"

"Paige happened. And you should talk, you're not Mr. Flexible either."

Gryff frowned. "Not anymore." But his brother was right.

"You can't let your past mistakes control your future," Grae told him.

Okay, fine, but... "Can we get back to the subject at hand?"

"You banging one of your associates?" Grae asked with a twitch of his lips.

"That's not the problem." Gryff's frown deepened. "Well, that's a slight problem. But not like the other one."

"Other one?" Grae asked, his eyebrows knitted together.

"Yeah."

"Okay, what's really bothering you?"

Gryff groaned and rubbed his palms over his face then scrubbed a hand over his short hair before stopping directly in front of his brother and facing him. He opened his mouth but nothing came out.

"Spill it."

"I had a threesome the other night."

Grae's eyebrows shot up his forehead. "What?"

"Yeah."

"Okay. And what's the problem?"

"It wasn't two women."

"Yes, I'm starting to figure out why you're being such a pansy and not getting to the point."

"We didn't have sex... Well..." Trey giving him head probably counted as sex. "Well, not... *Fuck.*"

Grae stared at the ceiling for a second, then his gaze dropped to the floor. "I'm not sure if I want to have this conversation with my younger brother," he muttered, clearly avoiding Gryff's eyes.

"That makes two of us, but I don't have anyone else to talk to about it."

Finally, Grae leveled his gaze at him. "And you're questioning the whole thing. Why?"

It was Gryff's turn to look away when he asked, "What if I like it?"

"Like what?"

"Being with another... man."

Grae laughed, whacking Gryff on the back and handing him the gin and tonic that sat untouched on the counter. "So what if you do?"

Gryff waved it away. His brother had a penchant for that nasty drink. He didn't. "Does that mean I'm gay?"

Grae stared at his brother for a moment, his face suddenly blank. Then he took a long sip of the drink before asking, "Am I gay?"

Gryff paused and frowned. "Fuck. I don't know. Are you?"

Grae shook his head. "I'm bisexual. But I don't give a damn what you call me. They're only words. I know how I feel about Paige. About Connor. I know how they feel about me. That's all that matters. Other people's opinions don't. Remember that."

"While that all sounds great, I head a law practice."

"And?"

"I have a reputation to uphold."

Grae's laughter filled the room. "Get over yourself."

He looked at his brother in surprise. "Like you did?"

"Yes, like me. Being with Paige and Connor is the best thing that ever happened to me. So, yes, I got over myself. And, little brother, you are the last person who should judge anyone."

"Thanks for the reminder."

"Somebody has to remind you to stay humble."

"Right. I already have a reminder of when I stopped chasing that dragon. It's over my shoulders, remember? I see that reminder every day in the mirror."

"Did they ask you about it?"

"No."

"Are you going to tell them?"

"No reason to at this point. We hooked up, that's all."

Grae cocked an eyebrow. "Right. So, you don't plan on seeing the guy again? Exploring your sexuality?"

"I have no choice but to see him." All thanks to Grae for dropping Trey directly in his path.

Grae's eyes narrowed, and he tilted his head. "Why's that?"

Gryff closed his eyes, embarrassed to admit who it was to his brother. "It's Trey Holloway."

He could have heard a pin drop. The silence became deafening until Gryff finally murmured, "Shit."

He opened his eyes and pinned Grae with a stare. "This is your fault."

"My fault? I asked you to represent him. Not fuck him."

Gryff sucked in a breath. "I didn't fuck him."

"*Yet.* Believe me, I know Trey. I know how he can charm the pants off any man or woman. I'm surprised you fell for it."

"I didn't fall for anything."

Grae shot him a look. "Did you get naked? Did she get naked? Did he get naked? Enough said." He pushed himself off the counter. "No, not enough said. How the hell did he get you to even agree with it? Where were you?"

"His apartment."

"His *apartment.* That penthouse he calls an *apartment?* So, he was slick enough to talk you over to his place."

Heat rushed into Gryff's face. Yeah, he may be dark and the blush not so apparent but his brother being just as dark, recognized embarrassment when he saw it. *Fuck.*

"You know, I don't have a problem with you exploring your wild side, because I'm sure you won't let it get out of hand like last time, but, brother, it's who you chose to do it with that worries me. Now I know why you mentioned being concerned about your reputation. Normally nobody would care who your bed partner or partners were since you're the best damned defense attorney out there. But now you're talking a player—and when I say player, I don't mean one who carries a ball, I mean *player*—who is front and center. And not just from football, from this latest arrest, too."

"So, what do I do?"

"Have your fun. Explore. Keep your mind open. And don't lie to yourself about it, either. See if it's what you want or need and then find it elsewhere. Kick his ass to the curb so he can go crawl up someone else's. Look, he's a great player. He's great for the Bulldogs. But I don't want to sit across from him at Thanksgiving. I don't. He can be trouble and you don't need trouble. He's not someone you bring home to Mom and Dad."

"I'm not interested in anything long term, anyway."

"Good. But what about this new attorney of yours? Rayne, is it? Even though you like her, she's still an employee."

"Unless I make her a partner."

Grae arched a brow. "You've never made anyone partner."

"She's good."

"As an attorney or in bed? Don't let your muddled mind mess with you. Great sex will do that."

"She's a brilliant defense attorney. She may be better than me."

"Damn," Grae whispered.

"Because of that, I put her on Holloway's case. That's where this all got jacked."

"No, *you* allowed it to get jacked. They're *your* employee, *your* client. I'm sure the two of them would have been fine hooking up without you getting involved."

Something rushed through him that he didn't like. And it sure felt like a little bit of jealousy with a tinge of loss of control. He shouldn't let his emotions control him. He was better than that. He had to *do* better than that.

Right.

"Your silence is telling, Gryff. You're trying to control your expression, but you can't. I know you well enough to recognize your jealousy." Grae shook your head. "You really are jacked. Let me show you why. Answer the following questions…"

Gryff frowned. *Great.* He wanted advice, not a damn lecture like Grae was his father.

"You want this woman?"

"Yes."

"She wants you?"

"Yes."

"She wants Trey?"

"Yes."

"Trey wants you?"

"Yes."

"Trey wants Rayne?"

"Yes."

"You want Trey?"

Gryff hesitated.

"Think long and hard on that. Be honest with yourself."

"*Fuck.*"

Grae's lips curled and his eyes crinkled at the corners. "That's what I thought. So, do what you have to do. Trey won't mind you using him to figure it out. He's got no hang-ups. I don't know Rayne, so I can't speak for her. Have fun. Then make sure you scrape him off afterward. I'll repeat; no holiday gatherings. I don't want to see him eating Mom's homemade sweet potato pie across from me. I swear, brother, don't mess that up."

Gryff sucked in a breath and nodded.

"By the way, you need to find someone else in the firm to represent him."

Gryff closed his eyes for a moment and sighed. "If I do this."

"*If* you do it," Grae repeated with a knowing grin.

"I already handed him off to Rayne. But now we'll have to find another associate to take the lead."

"The two of you can be advisors, because, believe me, we need to get this cleared up as soon as possible. Right now he can't even attend practices. Do your best to get the charges dropped. Convince the ADA that this was all a mistake."

"A mistake."

"Yes. You know all about mistakes—"

"What the fuck—"

Luckily, Paige wandered in before things got heated, because he didn't need Grae to keep bringing up his past transgressions. He knew his brother was trying to make a point... Which was to not make a mistake with Trey. But, really, there was no need to keep rubbing his nose in it. At this point in his life, he was way beyond making youthful mistakes.

Paige gave both of them a big smile and plastered herself to Grae's side, but not before standing on her tiptoes to plant a kiss on his brother's lips.

Gryff couldn't help but notice the way Grae's eyes softened when he looked at her. And his hand automatically slid to her hip, to hold her tight against him.

Her eyes bounced from Gryff to Grae and back. "Damn, I've said it before... Looking at the two of you is like looking at twins."

Grae shot her a scowl. "And like I told *you* before... Don't get any ideas."

She patted his stomach and laughed. "Don't worry, honey. Between you and Connor, I'm plenty busy. I don't need to add to my man sandwich." She pinned Gryff with a look. "So, what's the big discussion about?"

"Gryff's about to get fucked," his brother volunteered.

Gryff groaned.

CHAPTER 6

Gryff groaned as his cell phone lit up and a certain person's—who happened to be the one he was trying to avoid—name came up.

Why did he even program that number into his phone? Why did he even want the temptation?

He could ignore the call, or... He grimaced at his lack of willpower as he swiped his finger across the screen. "What."

"Damn, that's not a very friendly greeting."

"I could have ignored the call." *And you. And went back to my formally normal life.*

Silence greeted him.

"What do you want?" he demanded, not having the patience to deal with Trey this morning.

"I was just talking to Rayne—"

Of course you were.

"And she said you'll have to assign another attorney to my case."

"That's correct."

"Why?"

He lowered his voice since his office door was wide open. "Because we saw each other naked."

"Yeah. And?"

"And yeah."

"Is it illegal?"

"Let's just say it's extremely frowned upon."

"Okay, so then we're good."

"No. I'm good. You're not. You're still in a jam."

"Yeah, but you and Rayne will get me out of that."

"No promises."

"Okay, how about promising me that you two will still represent me."

"The five-hundred K retainer was only for one of us."

Silence again. Then a low whistle. "So, a cool mil for both of you."

"You don't need both of us," Gryff corrected him.

"I need both of you."

Gryff didn't think he was talking legal representation anymore.

He sighed, leaned back in his chair and stared at the ceiling. "Look, Trey, I'm one of the top firms in the area. I'd like to keep it that way by not getting involved in any type of ethical dilemma."

"I get it. You have a spotless reputation and I'm a spot," Trey answered quietly.

What the fuck. Now he felt... bad.

Though, he shouldn't. Trey probably only played him by using the "poor me" card. There was no reason to feel sorry for an overpaid sports figure.

"I need the best," Trey said.

"Anyone who represents you from my firm will be the best."

"But you'll stick me with someone else."

"You won't be stuck, you'll have one of my well-qualified, well-experienced associates to negotiate on your behalf. And we'll advise them."

"All because I saw you two naked."

"Well—"

"Okay, because my dick slipped into Rayne and my tongue slipped in your mouth and around your dick."

Gryff closed his eyes and pinched the bridge of his nose. *"Jesus.* Yes. Yes. Yes. That's why, Trey. Yes. Because of that."

"What if it doesn't continue?"

Gryff's eyes popped open in surprise. Wait a minute... "What?"

"What if it never happens again?"

He was not expecting that. And he also wasn't expecting his own reaction to those words. He frowned. He should be elated. But he wasn't.

Trey continued, "Yeah, we'll just keep it professional."

Gryff suddenly remembered the press of Trey's lips on his, their tongues meeting, tangling. "Well, uh—"

"It's probably what you want, anyway."

He pictured Trey on his knees, sucking him until he came down the man's throat. "I, uh—"

Trey chuckled in his ear. "See? I knew you wanted me."

"Fuck you, Trey," Gryff muttered and jabbed the End button on his cell. He tossed the phone onto his desk blotter and stared at it, scowling.

After his discussion with Grae, he actually considered exploring that side of himself to see if it was simply Trey that turned him on or men in general. He wanted to know if he was truly bisexual or heterosexual. Being in his mid-thirties, you'd think if it was men in general, he would have had a reaction before. Maybe he had and ignored it. Trey made himself hard to ignore.

Gryff even went as far as pulling some gay porn up on his laptop that night to see what his reaction would be. He discovered while it hadn't turned him off, it didn't completely do it for him either. It seemed to be Trey that did it for him. His body clearly reacted to the quarterback.

He guessed that was no different from his reaction with women, though. Rayne turned him on instantly. Dani, not at all. All women didn't turn him on. All men didn't turn him on.

Rayne.

Trey.

Fuck.

Gryff leaned his head back against the leather headrest of his office chair and closed his eyes. Memories of the other night's activities played in his mind like a movie. When he got to the part where Trey fucked Rayne over the end of the couch, he realized that had turned him on the most. And still did.

The evidence grew in his lap. His body was a traitor.

However, now he couldn't shake that image from his mind. He needed to clear that memory. Maybe replace it with a new one.

He pushed to his feet in a hurry, yanked at his tie to loosen it slightly, then rushed out the door. "I have a meeting with Rayne about the Holloway case," he announced to Dani in passing. "Hold my calls."

Gryff didn't wait for a response, his long legs eating up the real estate between him and Rayne's office. As he pushed open her door, he had a fleeting thought of how he needed to install locks on the private offices.

She looked up in surprise at his abrupt entry and covered the mouthpiece of the phone she held to her ear.

"Need something, Boss?"

The B word shot lightning down to his balls. Gryff's gaze narrowed in on the cleavage that mounded out of her blouse. Why she didn't button up the last few buttons, he'd never know. He would have to talk to her about it. All that flesh on display was inappropriate for his office. He would have to make sure she complied with the dress code.

Even though there wasn't a dress code.

He'd have to make one up.

Because no one else should get the eyeful he was. Only him.

Fucking damn.

"Boss?"

Gryff slowly lifted his eyes to her amused green ones.

"Who are you on the phone with?"

"A client."

"Who?"

Her eyes avoided his for a moment as she pointed her gaze to the window behind him.

So telling.

"Trey," he answered for her.

"Yes."

"Billable time?"

She hesitated, still avoiding his gaze. "No. I'll hang up."

He stepped around her desk and snagged the phone from her and said to Trey, "I should have known you'd call her back after talking to me."

His low chuckle grated on his nerves.

"If you're calling her at the office, then those will be billable hours. Do you understand?"

"Yes."

"But since you're on the phone, stay on the phone. I want you to listen to something important."

Gryff cut off his "What?" by jabbing the speaker button and hanging up the handset.

"Can you hear me?" he asked Trey.

"Yes. What's this about?"

"Just stay on the line."

No answer. But Gryff didn't care. He knew Trey would do just that.

He moved his attention back to Rayne. Grabbing her wrist, he pulled her out of her chair to her feet. She wobbled on her ridiculously high heels, but he caught her with an arm around her back, pulling her smack against him.

"You feel that?" he asked, his voice low, gravelly, looking down into her eyes. She didn't avoid his gaze now.

"Yes."

"Yes, what?" No, now she met his eyes and held them.

"Yes, Boss. I feel you." Her words came out on a breath and her nipples pebbled noticeably under her snug blouse.

"What you're wearing is inappropriate for this office. I want you to take it off."

"Make me."

Fuck. His cock jerked at her defiance. His mind spun and his fingers twitched with the urge to just rip open her blouse and let the tiny pearl buttons fly. However, he still had enough reasoning left in his bloodless brain to realize that would be hard to explain when she left the office. He doubted she kept extra clothes here.

"Take off your blouse or you will leave here today in nothing but your bra."

He heard a noise from the direction of the phone but he ignored it.

"You'd like that, wouldn't you? You'd like for me to strut down the hall in nothing but my panties and bra, wearing my high heels. You'd love for all the other men in this office to watch me do it. You'd love to have them all fuck me with their eyes and masturbate to the memory later that night. Is that what you want, Boss?"

Ah, fuck. No. No, that's not what he wanted. He wanted her all to himself. He didn't want anyone else to see her naked. Or even in her lingerie. And those heels of hers made her legs look endless. Legs that needed to be wrapped only around him as he thrust into her—

"I don't want anyone else to see her like that but us, Gryff," came from the phone.

"Shut up," he muttered to Trey as he realized Rayne just messed with his head.

"So, if you want me to undress, you do it."

"Are you going to fight me?" God, his balls couldn't get any tighter, his cock any harder.

"Absolutely."

"Fuck! Can you wait until I get there?" Trey yelled through the phone.

"No!" they both answered in unison.

"What the fuck! I can't listen to this. I want to be there."

"I'll hang up the phone if you don't shut up, Trey," Gryff warned without breaking Rayne's defiant, but glittering eyes. She enjoyed this.

But then, he did, too.

His lips tilted up at the corners. "You must not value that blouse then."

"I love this blouse."

"But you love getting fucked more."

"And I keep a change of clothes here. Just in case."

"Just in case your blouse gets ripped off?"

"That hasn't happened yet, Boss."

Gryff twisted the emerald-colored satin fabric in his fingers and yanked. She gasped, her torso jerking with the pull as buttons flew onto the floor, over her desk, pinging off the phone and the wall.

"Fuck. Me," Trey groaned.

Her chest heaved under his gaze as more of her cleavage came into view. He tugged the blouse from the waistband of the pencil skirt that hugged her curves and when he went to push it off her shoulders, she knocked his hands away. He reached again and she grabbed his wrists and held them away.

She wanted to play rough. She gave him a wicked smile that made his heart pound, his blood rush.

"You know what happens to naughty women?"

"No, what?" she asked, then bit her bottom lip.

Gryff almost groaned, but he caught it before it escaped. "You'll find out if you keep resisting."

"Sounds like a challenge, Boss," she said, her voice husky, low, driving him mad.

"Turn around."

"No."

Fuck. Me, Gryff echoed Trey. He grabbed her hips and spun her, and before she could fight him, he yanked the zipper of her skirt down and shoved it down to her ankles.

"Holy fuck," he murmured.

"What?" Trey yelled.

"She's wearing thigh-high stockings."

Trey groaned loudly. "I hate you. I'm going to hang up. I can't take anymore."

"Don't you dare," Gryff growled, unable to pull his gaze from her luscious thighs wrapped in sexy stockings. He was definitely not removing those. No fucking way. Because he planned on running his tongue around the lacy tops if it was the last thing he did.

And it just might be since all his blood had rushed south and pooled in his cock.

"Are those inappropriate, too?" she asked over her shoulder.

Oh, yes. Yes, they are. But he couldn't form the words. There was no blood left in his brain. Instead, his fumbling fingers unclipped her bra and before it could fall forward, she caught it and held it to her, keeping her breast covered.

"Let it go, Rayne."

"No."

With a rush of adrenaline, he swept his arm across her desk, knocking most of the items onto the floor. He sat on the edge and yanked her over his lap, and before she could react, he smacked her bare ass. That's right, bare. Because the woman hadn't even worn panties today.

So inappropriate.

He smacked his palm against her flesh once more and she gasped at the stinging contact and struggled in his lap, which did not help his erection. At all.

He heard a strange noise come from the phone which had been pushed to the edge of the desk. He could have sworn it was a whimper.

Each ass cheek now sported a red mark. He swore his head was going to blow off. Both the one attached to his neck and the one attached to his dick. He traced his fingertip over the thick lace band at the top of her stockings. He ran a finger underneath it and snapped it, then leaned over and kissed each cheek.

"What are you doing?" came the strangled question from the object he might have to smash into pieces.

"Wouldn't you like to know," Gryff mumbled.

"Is her ass pink? Oh, fucking fuck! Can we at least Skype?"

"No."

"Oh, you suck, Gryff. This is so unfair."

"Then hang up."

Silence. *Yeah. Thought so.*

He slipped a finger along the crease of her ass and through her slick folds. She was soaking wet.

"Let me go," she finally said, wiggling across his lap. *Jesus,* if she continued to do that, he'd lose it in his pants.

"Beg me."

"Please, Boss, let me go."

"Not until you come first."

"But I don't want to come," she whined.

Damn, he liked this game. "No?"

"No," she answered, then gasped as he slid two fingers into her.

"You don't like that?"

"No."

"No, what?"

"No, Boss."

A groan slipped from Gryff's lips as she tightened around his fingers. He pressed his thumb against her clit and circled it until she squirmed over his lap, then ground her hips against his.

He wouldn't last long like this. Leaning over, he sank his teeth into her ass cheek and she cried out, squeezing him tight. He felt a gush of warmth before she convulsed around his fingers, crying out once again.

"Oh, my God, did she come? Gryff! Did she come? Rayne, did you come?"

Gryff was so hard that it was painful and with Rayne's beautiful, just-orgasmed body draped over his lap, he was afraid to move. Literally, afraid to even breathe. But they weren't done yet. Not in the least. He needed to sink deep inside her to wash away that memory of Trey doing the same thing. He wasn't done torturing Trey yet, either.

He should be ashamed at his perverse pleasure of tormenting the man. But he wasn't.

"Stand up," he told her and helped her to her feet. Her face was flushed, her reddish-blonde hair a wild mane, and her bottom lip looked red and puffy as if she had been biting it. Oh, but he wanted to bite it instead.

"Come here," he murmured, snagging her wrists and pulling her to him. He captured her lips with his, licking that bottom lip of hers, soothing it with his tongue before dipping it inside her mouth, exploring.

"What are you doing now?" Trey shouted from the phone.

He yanked the bra from her hands and pinched both of her nipples, twisting them between the pads of his fingers. She moaned into his mouth. Then bit his bottom lip. He jerked away in surprise and pain.

"I'm not going to make this easy for you," she said, her eyes hooded, unfocused. Her breathing shallow.

"You better not," he agreed with a smile. He wiped his lip and noticed a tinge of red on his fingers.

Unfastening his belt, then his pants, he pulled his cock from his boxer briefs. He fisted himself once, then stood. "I'll show you who's boss."

"Holy fuck," came the groan from the phone. "I'm so fucking hard right now. This is so unfair. So unfair."

"I'll fuck you until you beg me to stop."

"Not going to happen," she said, backing away slowly.

"Which part? The fucking or the begging me to stop?"

"Both."

Gryff rushed her, pushing her back into the wall. Her breath left her in a rush. He pinned her there, grabbed behind her thighs and lifted her legs up and around his waist.

She released a low laugh until he drove deep inside her on the first thrust. Then she cried out, arched her back and closed her eyes. He fucked her against the wall, pounding her hard, deep and relentlessly. He wouldn't be surprised if he had to have the drywall patched after the impact.

"What are you doing? What's going on?" came Trey's impatient voice.

Little mews of pleasure escaped her lips every time he hit the end of her and couldn't go any further.

"Is that too much for you, Rayne?" he grunted.

"No. Give me more."

"You can't take anymore."

"Fucking give it to me. I want it."

He dug his fingers into the flesh of her ass, her weight held up by his strength and the wall. He took long, deep strokes, feeling her insides hug him tight, get slicker by the second. Squeeze, release.

He was going to lose his mind. Her arms wrapped around his neck, one hand pushing his head closer and he kissed her thoroughly, roughly. He conquered her mouth until both of them were breathing too hard to keep their lips sealed together. He pulled away just enough to drop his forehead to hers, his breath ragged, his heart pounding out of his chest. His balls squeezing tight, his cock becoming as hard as steel. He was about to blow.

"Tell me when you're going to come."

"I'm going to come," yelled Trey.

"Not you, asshole," Gryff yelled. Then he dropped his head and sucked a nipple between his lips, scraped the tip with his teeth and she cursed while her hips did a little dance against him.

He was becoming unraveled and wanted to release inside her... like yesterday. But he had to wait. He had to hold off. Just a little while longer. He could do it.

He shoved a hand between them and tweaked her clit, then rubbed it furiously until she made a sound that just about made him blow his load. Her hips rocked against him, grinding him deeper inside her.

Her wet heat hugged him, then he felt it change, ripple, her G-spot hardened, and he knew he was in the clear. She was about to climax.

Thank fucking God.

"Tell me."

"No."

He wanted to laugh but he couldn't. "Tell me."

"No."

Now he wanted to cry. She would fight him until the end. "Tell me," he said thrusting even harder. So hard he was surprised they didn't crash through the wall into the next room, which, luckily, was a supply closet and not another associate's office. Because that would be awkward.

When she didn't answer him this time, he knew he had her. She was there. Then, she exploded around him, unable to contain her cry, unable to hide her body's response.

And *finally... Finally*, he let himself go. He released inside her, making her his once again.

Despite his arms and legs trembling, he continued to hold her tight against the wall. Not wanting to leave her, not wanting to separate. He wanted to remain one with her a moment longer. For as long as his body would allow it.

Which, unfortunately, wasn't long enough. As his dick decided enough was enough, he slipped from her. As he reluctantly released the hold he had on her ass, her feet finally touched the floor. He caught her when she wobbled against him and pressed his lips softly against her forehead, then her lips, before capturing her chin in his fingers and looking at her seriously.

"I'm sorry, this isn't a competition," he murmured.

She tilted her head slightly and studied him. "If I didn't want you to fuck me, I would say no."

"But, after the fact, I feel like I'm disrespecting you by taking you against the wall or bent over my office chair."

"Do I look offended? Or do I look satisfied?"

He studied her and then ran a knuckle down her flushed cheek. "You look like someone who's been thoroughly fucked."

"And that's not a bad thing."

"No, but next time I want us to take our time and enjoy each other."

"I enjoyed this."

"You don't want to have sex in a bed?"

"I'd like that, too. On the floor, on the bed, over your knee, in the shower. Any way you want to give it to me, Gryff, I won't say no. Unless you like it when I'm obstinate."

He smiled then. She was something else. "I like it when you're willing. I like it when you're fighting me. I'll take it any way you want to give it to me, Rayne."

"Me, too," came Trey's weary voice. Gryff was sure he found his own release while they found theirs.

"I almost forgot you were there, until you opened your big mouth."

"You'll never forget me, Gryff, admit it. Especially my big mouth."

"Fuck you, Trey," Gryff growled, and moved to the desk to pick up the receiver and slam it back on the base.

Rayne smothered her laugh. "That wasn't nice."

"I'm sure he got his rocks off."

"Wasn't that the point of putting him on speaker phone? Or was it just to rub this in his face?"

"Mostly the second part."

"Well, at least you're honest," she said pulling on her skirt and turning so he could zip it closed for her.

"That I am." Funny that how in the heat of the moment, he had no problem with that tiny zipper, but now? His fat fingers had the hardest time gripping the little zipper tab. He finally finished securing it, then snagged her before she could pull away. He lifted her hair up and kissed the back of her neck. Her smooth, delicate skin tasted slightly salty when the tip of his tongue darted out.

"Should I finish getting dressed or are we going for round two?"

With a sigh, he let her go, and glanced down at his flaccid dick, which still hung out of his pants. With a tug, he tucked it away and pulled up his underwear. "No. I need to get back to working on Peter Martin's case."

She nodded her head and when she turned as she secured her bra into place, she looked somewhat disappointed. "Can we do this again soon? And not in the office?"

"When do you have plans to hook up with Trey?"

He didn't miss when her expression changed, though, she quickly hid it from him. "I have no plans to meet up with him at this point."

"Why not?"

She shrugged, then picked her destroyed blouse up off the floor. She looked at it for a moment, then headed to her office closet. "Because you interrupted our conversation," she said, her back to him as she pulled a spare blouse off of a hanger. She shrugged it on and began to button it.

He wanted to see her face. "Rayne..."

"Boss?" she whispered, still refusing to turn.

"Were you going to make plans with him?"

Her shoulders lifted slightly and finally she turned around, her blouse closed. He realized all her lipstick was gone from their kissing and the pink in her cheeks was not makeup. Her natural look made his breath catch. This was what she would look like waking next to him in the morning. Hair mussed, face makeup free. Smoky green eyes watching him.

His heart squeezed, then resumed a heavy thumping. He had never wanted any kind of commitment from a woman. Nor did he ever want to commit.

Until now.

He wanted her.

And she wanted him. But not only him. Trey, too.

Either way, he had to accept that fact, or he had to fight for her. "Let me take you to dinner Friday night."

"You mean like an actual date?"

"Yes. Just me and you. I'll pick you up and escort you to one of the best restaurants in the city."

Her eyebrows rose. "It's impossible to get reservations this late in the week."

She was right. But that wouldn't deter him. "You let me worry about that."

His eyes dropped to the V of her blouse. This one was no better in covering her than the one he ripped off of her. He couldn't resist tracing a finger over the soft mounds of her flesh. Then he curled his fingers into fists and stepped away, heading toward the door. "I'm going to draft a dress code."

"You better not."

Gryff opened the door and chuckled as he shut it behind him. He leaned against the door for a second and blew out a breath. Then straightened his spine as he snapped back into work mode.

As he walked past Dani's desk, she asked, "Is everything all right? It sounds like that *meeting* got a little heated."

Gryff kept his expression blank. "We just disagreed on the course of action in Holloway's case, that's all."

"Well, hopefully you got everything worked out," she said with a smirk.

"We did," he assured her and rushed into his office, keeping the door shut for the rest of the afternoon.

CHAPTER 7

Gripping the bouquet of Calla Lilies tightly, Gryff rang her doorbell. He was actually nervous. Nervous. Him!

He felt like a teenager picking up his prom date. With a quick glance down, he assessed his outfit just to make sure he had his shit together. Ironed, matched and tucked, he looked good. At least his mirror had said so.

He tried to go for a more casual look tonight, wearing an eggplant dress shirt that emphasized the deep tone of his skin, no tie, no jacket. He even left a couple of the top buttons undone. A pair of black slacks, freshly shined shoes and he went as far as slipping a diamond earring into his left ear. Something he never wore to work. The holes in his ears had never closed up since he had them pierced in his youth, and sometimes when he wanted to be on the more "wild" side, he'd dig out his half carat stud. One, but never both.

When the door cracked open, he was blinded for a moment. Not from the foyer light, no. From the beauty of the woman before him. Her hair fell around her bare shoulders softly, looking a little more tamed than usual, her green eyes appeared smoky, her lips glossy, her cheeks a healthy pink. She wore a slip of a dress. And that's exactly what it looked like... a slip. Spaghetti straps held up a loose sheath that only clung to her breasts, her outer hips and, he assumed, the ripe globes of her ass. He couldn't see behind her yet, but he'd make it a point to get a glimpse shortly. Her nipples were unmistakable under the green fabric that matched her eyes. In fact, he didn't think she even wore a bra. The bottom hem barely hit mid-thigh and it had six inch slits up both sides.

In fact, this looked like something she'd wear to bed at night. A sexy nightie. *What the fuck.* She couldn't wear that out to dinner.

No fucking way.

If she was his woman, she'd never leave the house like that. Around the house? Yes. She could wear that all day long. At least until he tore it off her before throwing her on the bed.

"Are you just going to stand there? Or are you coming in?" Amusement lit up her eyes, and he realized he'd stared at her like a lost soul. His mouth had gone dry, and he desperately needed a drink... One with alcohol.

As she stepped back to let him cross the threshold, he realized this was the first time he'd seen her not wearing heels. Hell, without any shoes at all. She seemed so much more petite without them.

She closed the door behind him and then led him down the hallway.

His eyes glued to the thin spaghetti straps that crisscrossed the smooth length of her bare back. That ass, though... Nothing petite about it.

He didn't get to see much of her condo before they ended up in her kitchen at the back of the house. It was open and modern and—

What the fuck.

"Our reservation is at seven."

She spun to face him and snagged the flowers out of his hands. "Cancel it," she said, while digging through a nearby cabinet for a vase, then filling it with water at the sink. She ripped the paper off the base of the flowers and plunged them into the water before turning toward him again. Where he stood frozen like a dumbass.

He had done some groveling to get that reservation and now she wanted him to cancel?

That's when he noticed the delicious smell in the air and the pots on the stove. "You cook?"

She placed the flowers in the center of the kitchen table and then faced him with her hands on her hips. Which made him appreciate that small waist of hers sandwiched between generous curves. Suddenly, he wasn't so upset about the wasted reservation.

"Why are you so surprised?"

Good question. "I, uh—"

"I'm multi-talented," she continued with a smile on her face.

That he would not argue with.

"I'll have to say we got into a bad car wreck, otherwise I'll never get reservations there again. I bribed the maître d'."

"Where did you get them?"

"La Fourchette D'Or."

"Oh." She moved quickly to the stove and peeked into one of the pots. She dipped a wooden spoon in and Gryff watched in fascination as her tongue darted out to taste whatever lucky food clung to the utensil. Something twitched in his pants. "Sorry, my cooking doesn't even compare to the chefs at La Fourchette. I don't want to disappoint you..."

"Will it kill me?"

She looked at him over her shoulder in surprise. "What? No." Then she laughed. One of those husky, sexy, *oh, fuck-me* laughs that made him swallow hard. "I sure hope not. I've never killed anyone with my cooking before." Her voice dropped even lower. "But there's always a first time."

She was killing him right now.

He pushed away the chauvinist thought of how sexy she looked standing in the kitchen in front of the stove wearing that... whatever it was, barefoot and braless, cooking him a meal. He couldn't remember the last time a woman went through the trouble to make him dinner. Well, a woman other than his mother.

Most women he dated wanted to be wined and dined. But this woman seemed to be the total package. Wicked smart, successful, absolutely stunning, and she could do more than pick up a phone to order takeout.

Fighting Trey for her was looking better and better. Which, again, sounded a little chauvinistic and juvenile. But damn...

He moved behind her at the stove and wrapped his arms around her waist, pulling her against his chest. He leaned his chin on her shoulder. "What are you making?"

"Can you figure it out?" she asked, sliding a hand around the back of his neck and leaning her head back to rest against his shoulder.

He couldn't resist moving his hands up her belly until he cupped her breasts. He nuzzled her neck, then lightly sucked on her skin. When she shivered, her nipples peaked under his fingers. He rubbed the silky fabric back and forth across them with his thumbs. Just as he expected. No bra. And now that they were staying in, he appreciated the fact. Even though, he might be distracted during dinner.

"I'm starving," he murmured into her ear. "I can't wait to eat." He was *not* talking about food.

He felt the vibration of her chuckle rather than heard it, and he smiled into her hair.

"You haven't guessed what I'm making yet."

Honestly, if it was up to him, they could skip dinner and he would gladly go without food. She alone could sustain him.

But to make her happy, his gaze swept the stove top and the nearby counters. "I can smell the garlic and the shrimp."

"I hope you don't mind. I love garlic."

"I do, too. And as long as we both taste like garlic, neither can be offended, right?"

"Right. I'm glad you're of the same mindset."

His eyes landed on the nearby stainless steel pasta maker. She made pasta from scratch. *Holy hell.*

"Lift that lid. I can't seem to move my hands right now," he said, his fingers continuing their massage of her breasts over the slip. He couldn't imagine it wasn't a slip or a nightie because what she wore couldn't be an actual dress. He realized that now. Because, once again, his thought was that there would be no way in hell he'd allow her to go out in public wearing it.

He grimaced. He might as well start grunting like the caveman he acted.

Fuck.

She released one hand from around the back of his neck and lifted a lid. He leaned forward slightly, bringing her with him. Then she lifted another lid.

His mother didn't raise no fool. He was definitely not letting Trey sweep her away from him. Not ever.

"Homemade pasta. A white sauce which certainly looks like Alfredo. Steamed veggies. Yes. I'm impressed. You're multi-talented. I'll give you that."

His erection pressed into the crease of those luscious ass cheeks. He did his damnedest not to thrust. He didn't want to risk her getting burned on the stove.

"Do we have time for you to come sit on my lap quick before dinner is done?"

She laughed. "Only if you want burnt Alfredo sauce, soggy pasta, and rubbery shrimp."

"Is it awful if I say I don't mind risking it?"

"Yes, Boss. It is."

Gryff groaned. "Oh. Fuck. Me. Don't call me that right now."

"Okay, Boss," she answered, humor in her voice.

He stepped back quickly before dinner went south... and so did he. He paced to the other side of the kitchen, needing to cool off.

Which would be impossible if he continued to touch her, or even look at her.

His cock was so hard right now that it was painful. Maybe he should excuse himself to relieve it. Just a quick—

No. No. No.

He had more control than that. What kind of man excuses himself to go to the bathroom to jerk off? Someone without self-control. That was not him. He had fought long and hard to take control of his life, to make his way to the top. To be reduced to an asshole without any control made him no better than what he escaped. It made him no better than someone like Trey. A cocky shit who did whatever he wanted and be damned with the consequences.

He was not like that anymore. He would never go back to being like that ever again. He slayed that dragon once.

But damn, his dick just had a mind of its own.

"You okay?" she asked.

"Just a little muscle cramp."

"I'm not sure it could be considered a muscle."

He strode back to her, pulled the wooden spoon out of her hand, thrusting his hands into her hair, and took her mouth like he owned it.

She whimpered, grabbing his biceps, opening her lips to him, allowing him complete control.

This wasn't helping his situation out at all. Not. At. All.

He pulled back enough to say, "I appreciate the effort you went through to make this meal from scratch. Believe me, I do. I'm humbled, in fact. But how soon can we eat and get it over with?"

She bit her bottom lip, her eyes unfocused as she stared at his mouth.

"Keep that up and that sauce will be burnt to the bottom of the pot," he warned, releasing her and stepping back. Again.

"Can you pour the wine?"

Oh hell yes. That's what he needed. Booze. Something to dull the edge. He closed his eyes at the sudden image of sucking red wine from her belly button.

Jesus fuck. He was losing it. "Why did you have to wear that? Why didn't you wear a damn track suit?"

"Maybe because I don't own one?"

He groaned at his own suffering and looked around the kitchen for the wine. Something, anything, to get his mind off her. Even for a moment.

"Wine's on the table," she mentioned. "Glasses are already on the table, too."

Obviously, he thought, his mind clouded. She had already set the table before he got there.

But wait...

He froze and without turning, he asked, "Why are there three place settings?"

Oh fuck no.

Fuck. No.

No wonder she wanted him to cancel the reservation.

"Please tell me you don't know how to count," he said, staring at the third setting.

"I know how to count."

He opened his mouth and turned but before anything could come out the doorbell rang. His spine stiffened.

Oh fuck no.

"Can you get that?"

"Rayne…" He blew out a breath. "You really don't want me to get that right now. Trust me." His fingers curled into fists.

That was definitely not a good idea.

It turned out that no one had to let him in. Trey being Trey let himself in. And he came directly back to the kitchen...

Like he'd been there before and already knew the layout of the condo. When he entered the kitchen, it took everything Gryff had to not lay the fucker out.

"Have you been here before?"

Trey halted just inside the doorway, his eyes finding his, his expression quickly masked. "What kind of greeting is that?"

"It was either that or my fist."

"Gryff—"

Gryff cut him off. "No. Answer the question."

When Trey's eyes cut to Rayne, he knew the answer.

"So, it's okay that you get to fuck her whenever you want. But me? No. You don't like it. Well, tough shit, Gryff. It's not your say. It's Rayne's."

"Both of you!" Rayne shouted, wielding the wooden spoon. "Sit the fuck down at the table and act civilized. I'm not a piece of meat. Don't treat me as such. Now... Sit. The. Fuck. Down." She pointed the spoon at one end of the table. "You, there." She pointed the spoon at the opposite end. "You, there. And if either of you move toward each other, you get it with the spoon. Do you hear me?"

Gryff sank into the chair he was banished to, Trey doing the same. The other man's eyes narrowed as he stared at him from across the table.

Gryff glared back, judging the distance.

"Don't even think about it," came her warning from the stove. "I swear to God, if either of you do something stupid, neither of you will get laid. And I didn't wear this and make dinner for nothing."

Then Trey smirked. And Gryff relaxed. Well, for the most part. He still had a raging hard-on. Not caring who saw him, he adjusted it to a more comfortable position.

"Problem?" Trey asked, his smirk widening into a grin.

"You."

"I gave you that? I'm flattered."

"Have you ever had a cock this big in your ass?"

"Bigger."

Rayne slapped something on the counter and both of them jumped. "I worked hard on this dinner. Don't ruin it."

Gryff finally tore his gaze away from the man across from him to see Rayne standing there upset.

Damn it.

He had looked forward to this date with her. Their first date. And now he was ruining it. No. Correction. Trey was ruining it.

"Fuck you, Trey," he said under his breath.

"I look forward to it," Trey mouthed back.

"Can someone help—"

Before she could finish the request, both of them were out of their seats rushing to help her.

"Stop!" she yelled and they slid to a stop, inches from each other. "Civilized, please. Like adults, not two dogs fighting over a bone." She held out a large bowl. "Trey, take this. Gryff, take the bread."

They did what they were told, side-eyeing each other the whole time. The food got to the table safely, and there wasn't any bloodshed by the time they settled into their seats, Rayne between them.

No one said a word as the food was passed. Until Trey swallowed his first forkful of her homemade Fettucine Alfredo. "Damn, baby, this is good. Even though I really only came for dessert."

Gryff ignored the last part, but agreed with how good the pasta dish was. Even the rolls were freshly baked.

Yeah, she was worth fighting Trey over. She wasn't going to slip through his fingers. He'd do whatever he needed to do.

CHAPTER 8

Rayne pushed her empty plate out of the way and looked at one man and then the other.

This was not going as planned. If she didn't take control now, she didn't think the three of them would even have a shot.

She knew Gryff was attracted to Trey, but he was being too stubborn to admit it. Obviously, Trey wanted Gryff, but he confessed to Rayne he wasn't sure if it was worth the grief.

She didn't blame him. She wondered that herself.

So, if things didn't go right tonight, she would have to step back and reevaluate. She might have to pick one or the other, and she didn't want to do that.

Just as stubborn as the two meatheads sitting at both ends of the table, she would make this work if it was the last thing she did.

Or someone got seriously injured. Or even died.

She frowned.

Trey snagged her chin and turned her to face him. "Don't frown, baby. Dinner was great, Gryff hasn't tried to kick my ass yet, we've kicked two bottles of wine, and it's still early."

"Yep. Night's not over. A good ass-kicking may be in the works yet."

Rayne closed her eyes, inhaling deeply. When she opened them, Trey's were soft and caring. "Thank you for dinner, baby."

She nodded, breaking his grasp, and turned toward Gryff. Waiting.

His dark eyes met hers and a second later they widened like he'd forgotten his manners. "Yes, thank you for dinner... *baby.*"

She sighed, trying desperately not to slam her palm on the table. "This is what's going to happen... I'm going to go upstairs with my glass of wine. To my bedroom. To my bed. I'm going to be waiting up there. Either still wearing this or possibly wearing nothing. While I'm waiting, both of you will clean up this mess. Put away the leftovers. Scrub the pots. Leave this kitchen spotless. No fighting. No blood. Nothing. Then when you're *both* done, you *both* will come up and find me. Then we will work this all out. I had hoped this would be accomplished during dinner. But, since no one talked that became a little impossible. So, now we're following my rules. My house, my rules. My bed, my rules. No exceptions. If you don't like my rules, you know where the door is. If you don't want to *share* my bed, you know where the door is. If I hear one argument, one tussle, one curse, I'm locking my bedroom door. Is this clear?"

"Crystal," Trey said, already standing and taking her plate away.

Rayne's gaze bounced to Gryff. "Boss?"

"Can I refill your glass?"

She smiled. "Yes, please."

As she made her way upstairs, she couldn't wipe off that smile even if she tried.

~

"W hy a defense attorney?" Trey asked, his hand deep in sudsy water as he scrubbed one of the pots. Alfredo sauce was a bitch to clean up. He would have dish-pan hands.

Next time, they just needed to throw some steaks and potatoes on the grill. Cleanup would be easy-peasy.

"Because I know what it's like to need one," Gryff said behind him. Trey couldn't get enough of his deep-timbre voice. He could listen to it all day. Or preferably, all night.

Even if the guy was being a stubborn shit.

"Really? I can't even imagine you getting a parking ticket." He wondered about the story behind that. But that thought quickly fled when Gryff set another pot next to the sink. "Another one?"

"Last one," Gryff assured him. "Hey, I wanted to take her out to dinner where someone else does the cleanup. This was not my ideal first date."

"First date?"

"Yeah, I know dating is probably a foreign concept to you. You probably just fuck your groupies in alleyways. Oh, wait. Behind bars."

"Seriously? You want to start with me and lock yourself out of her bedroom?"

Trey looked over his shoulder when he only received silence for an answer. Gryff stood staring at him. And not just looking through him, but really looking *at* him, studying. Trey wasn't sure if that was a good thing, or bad.

"If anyone is going to get locked out, it's you," Gryff finally answered.

"Why's that? Because once you go black, you don't go back?"

Gryff shook his head. "You did not just say that."

Yes, he did. It was stupid. He wasn't supposed to be starting a fight. Instead he should be encouraging Gryff to take the next step. But the man could be frustrating.

Trey never had to work so hard to get someone in his bed. He wondered, more than once, if it was even worth the effort.

"Like I asked before, have you ever had a cock this big in your ass?"

Trey chucked the sponge in the pot and turned to face Gryff. He wasn't sure how to answer him without pissing the other man off. And they needed to get past that. "Are you offering?"

93

Gryff's lips flat lined and he handed Trey the dishtowel.

After Trey wiped his hands off, he leaned back against the sink, crossing his arms over his chest. "Do you want to fuck me in the ass, Gryff?"

Gryff broke eye contact, grabbed his nearby glass and took a gulp of wine. Trey couldn't pull his eyes away from the thick, corded muscles convulsing in his throat as he swallowed.

Trey pushed away from the counter and moved behind Gryff. He reached around him, took the wine glass from his fingers and carefully placed it on the counter. He brushed a hand over Gryff's broad back, feeling the muscles bunch beneath his shirt. "Gryff," he said, his voice catching in his throat. "Do you want to fuck me?"

Gryff's head dropped forward and Trey skimmed a hand over his ass. The man was solidly built and took care of himself. Trey already knew that since he'd seen him naked in his apartment. Ever since then, he couldn't wait to see Gryff naked again. He couldn't stop thinking about touching and tasting his dark skin. All of it.

"Gryff," Trey whispered, sliding his hand around Gryff's hip to the front and discovering the proof he turned the man on. "Why do you fight it?"

Gryff shook his head slightly, his head still bowed.

"Why do you deny yourself?"

"I don't know," Gryff finally answered. His words raw, painful. To hear them squeezed Trey's heart.

"Is it because it's me? Because I'm not good enough? I'm not worthy?"

"What the fuck, Trey. No." He lifted his head, grabbed Trey's arm and pulled him around to face him. "No. It's not you. It's me. This is... I don't... I've never had this reaction to any man before. It's freaking me out a little. Hell, not a little, a lot."

Trey swallowed hard, understanding where the man was coming from. Finding out you're attracted to someone of the same sex hit everyone differently. Some accepted it easily. Some never accepted it and went their whole life denying themselves what they really wanted, what they needed to feel fulfilled.

Gryff seemed to be in the middle right now. Trey and Rayne both knew Gryff had that desire, otherwise she never would have pushed the issue tonight. Gryff knew he had the desire, otherwise he would have walked out that front door. But he didn't. *He didn't.* Instead he stood in the kitchen with Trey, letting another man touch him. If he had no attraction to Trey, Gryff never would have allowed it. Trey would have been knocked down and out. He was sure of it.

"Now that I'm in the vicinity of your fists, I'm going to ask first; Can I touch you?"

Gryff blinked once, twice, blew out a breath, then met his eyes. "Yes."

Trey's lips twitched. "Was that a difficult decision?"

"Don't push your luck," Gryff grumbled.

Trey lifted his palms in mock surrender then plastered them on Gryff's pecs, which flexed under his hands.

Damn. The man was powerful. No doubt. He could stand right beside him in the Bulldogs' locker room and put some of those guys to shame.

"I don't even know what to do," he muttered.

Trey moved closer, letting his hands slide down the man's abs. "The same as you would with a woman."

Gryff shook his head slowly. "Not quite the same."

"Close enough."

Trey slid one palm along Gryff's hard length, then placed his other hand along Gryff's cheek. They were the same height, which made it hard for Gryff to avoid Trey's eyes when they were so close.

"Look at me," Trey murmured.

Gryff's nostrils flared, but finally met his eyes. "You shaved."

Trey smiled. The man finally noticed. "Yes."

"You trimmed your hair."

"I did."

"Why?" Gryff asked softly.

"So I look a little more respectable."

"Why is that important to you?"

"It's not. I think it's important to you."

"Why do you care what I think?"

"Because I want you in my bed."

"You think shaving and trimming your hair will get me in your bed?"

"I'm hoping it'll get both of us in Rayne's bed tonight."

"Did you help her plan this?"

Trey leaned in until his lips were a hair's breadth from Gryff's. "Yes. Are you going to keep talking or can I kiss you now?"

"Why are you asking?"

"Because, I'd like to keep my lips attached to my face. They're usefu—"

Gryff cut him off, taking his mouth, pushing his lips apart with his tongue, then jamming it deep. Trey fought back, wanting to explore Gryff's mouth instead. He groaned, his hand finding Gryff's hot, heavy sac and cupping it over his pants. He squeezed softly, then stroked the hidden, hard length a couple times before Gryff's fingers tangled in Trey's T-shirt. Not pushing him away. No. Pulling him closer.

Trey struggled to breathe since Gryff dominated the kiss. He tried to pull back slightly, but the man wouldn't let him. He held him even tighter, shoving Trey back until he hit the counter behind him. Gryff pinned him, his hips pushing against him.

Trey finally shoved his hands between them and pushed him away enough to break the kiss, panting. "Damn, now that's what I'm talking about. I want it like that. You want to dominate, I'll let you. I want you any way I can get you."

Gryff's chest heaved with each deep breath he took. He seemed just as oxygen starved as Trey.

"I want to take you in my mouth again, but then we may never make it upstairs. And we really don't want to leave Rayne hanging."

"No, we don't," Gryff said slowly. "Trey…"

He could see the struggle on Gryff's face.

"It'll be all right. I promise. We'll take it slow. We won't do anything you don't want to do. Anything Rayne doesn't want to do. If we need to keep her between us tonight, we can. But, hear this, I won't have the patience for that very long. I want to touch you, I want you inside me."

Trey left off the part where he wanted to be inside Gryff, too. No point in freaking him out. Baby steps.

"Do you have—"

"Rayne has a lot of lube and condoms upstairs."

Gryff stepped back, letting Trey ease away from the counter. "How do you know that?"

Shit. "I dropped them off to be sure."

"So, the last time you were here, you didn't fuck her?"

"I didn't say that."

"*Jesus.*"

"Gryff, you fucked her while I listened on the phone."

"Yeah. And?"

"And yeah," Trey threw back at him. "At least I didn't call you and make you listen."

"No one forced you to listen."

"Yeah, but it was hot."

"And you came."

"I certainly did."

Gryff laughed. "Fuck you, Trey."

Trey smiled. "Rayne's waiting."

$\sim$

Tired of waiting, Rayne had lost all of her patience. After listening to the low voices downstairs, although they didn't sound raised in anger, she hoped they weren't bickering. As the moments ticked by and she didn't hear a slam of the front door, her optimism grew.

Then she heard their feet, heavy on the stairs. Two sets. Her heartbeat surged, and she trembled in both anticipation and nervousness.

She still wore the outfit she'd worn for dinner, wanting to leave a little something to their imagination. She ripped the nightstand drawer open to make sure that the lube and condoms Trey had brought over last time were still there. They were. They hadn't disappeared since the last twenty times she checked.

Should she feel guilty that Trey and she had gotten together without Gryff? She didn't think so. There were no rules for this sort of thing. Nothing set in stone. At least not yet. If things continued like the two of them hoped, if things moved forward with Gryff being willing, rules may need to be put in place. But for now, Gryff shouldn't have a problem with what Trey and she did a couple nights ago. Just like he didn't have a problem fucking her against the wall in her office to rub it in Trey's face.

She had left her bedroom door open and wondered who would be the first through the door.

Trey. He gave her a secret smile, along with a wink. Next, he'd be giving her a thumb's up and a high five.

Gryff followed close behind and when he stepped around Trey, he pinned her to the bed with his gaze. "You left it on."

"Yes. I figured you'd want to take it off me."

"Oh, wait. He gets to?" Trey said, approaching the bed, ripping his T-shirt over his head and tossing it aside. Rayne lost her breath and her train of thought for a moment. Trey, even though very muscular, was leaner than Gryff. His body was nothing short of spectacular, as a professional athlete's should be. Being low in body fat, every muscle rippled along his torso. The other night, she had explored each tattoo decorating his chest. Some had meaning, some didn't. He didn't regret even one.

The one that had caught her attention first had been the Boston Bulldog logo on his right pec over his heart. She had asked him what he would do if he couldn't get cleared of his charges and ended up kicked off the team permanently.

He had said, "I have faith in you and Gryff. Grae has faith in you two. You'll get me clear. I'll be back on the field soon."

She was glad he had such confidence, and she believed she'd get them to drop the charges, but the judge he drew was tough. She didn't look forward to going head to head with him. Or helping one of the other associates to go up against him, since Gryff didn't want him or her publicly standing up for Trey in the courtroom for obvious reasons.

When her eyes slid to Gryff, heat bloomed into her cheeks. He watched her checking out Trey. She was sure her expression left no doubt to what she'd been thinking.

"Now you," she told him, her voice husky.

She sat up straighter against the headboard while Gryff slowly unbuttoned his shirt.

Suddenly she yelled, "Stop!" and he hesitated halfway down his shirt. He looked at her with a question in his eyes. "Let Trey do it."

"I like how you think, baby," Trey said and approached Gryff, who stood in the center of the room, his arms now dropped to his side.

"Just don't block my view," she warned him.

Trey chuckled and after he finished unbuttoning the dress shirt, he pulled it from Gryff's waistband and moved behind him to slide it off his shoulders. He tossed it on a nearby chair, then reached around Gryff's waist, snagged the bottom of his undershirt and tugged that over his head. It landed somewhere near the chair.

"Like a piece of art, right?" Trey asked Rayne, brushing his fingertips over the hard curves of Gryff's abs.

Rayne couldn't answer. Having two scorching hot men in her condo, in her bedroom, and soon in her bed... she had to be dreaming. It seemed like the guys had come to some sort of understanding while they talked downstairs. Gryff didn't seem so uncomfortable. At least not yet.

"Shoes off. Socks off. Pants off. Hurry up," she demanded. Though her voice sounded a little too breathy to be bossy.

Trey's smile got wider, and the corners of Gryff's eyes crinkled, though he hadn't quite cracked a smile yet.

He would.

She was sure of it.

The differences in the men were obvious, of course. Gryff dark. Trey light. Gryff's hair tightly trimmed, Trey's, even though trimmed now, still a little shaggy. Gryff's eyes a dark, soul-searching brown. Trey's a bright sky blue. Gryff serious. Trey... not.

Trey tossed his clothes in a pile. Gryff neatly folded his and placed them on the chair.

Yin and Yang.

She was one lucky woman.

Both men's erections were long and thick. Trey stood a little bit behind Gryff and Rayne knew he studied the darker man. Taking his time, he ran his gaze over his shoulders, over that black dragon, down Gryff's solid back, the muscular globes of his ass, his thick thighs and defined calves. All while Gryff's attention remained on her.

"What's he doing?" Gryff asked her as if incapable of turning around.

"Appreciating your beauty," she said, giving him a reassuring smile.

"You're the one who's beautiful," he responded, making her heart squeeze at his words.

"Each of us are beautiful in different ways," she said. She completely understood why Trey made no move for the bed. She couldn't keep her eyes off Gryff, either. Each wanted to savor the moment.

"Are you just going to stand there, Trey?" Gryff finally asked, looking a little uncomfortable.

"No," he murmured. "I want to do so much more."

"Where do we start?"

Trey finally moved past Gryff to stand beside the bed. "With Rayne."

Gryff shook his head slightly, not quite understanding.

Trey explained, "Rayne is our center. We concentrate on her. We pleasure her. We share her. If you want to touch me during this, you touch me. If you want more, we do more. No need to ask me, just take what you want from me. I'm sure Rayne feels the same."

"Yes, whatever you want, Boss. Whatever feels good to you. To me. To Trey."

Trey continued, "If I forget myself and I do something you're not comfortable with, just simply tell me to stop. I don't want to risk doing anything that will make you not want to do this again."

Trey climbed on the bed and pulled Rayne to her knees, moving behind her. He kissed along her shoulders, sliding one of the thin straps out of the way. Lifting her hair, he kissed along her neck, then sucked at the skin at the top of her spine. A shiver ran through her.

He pressed his lips to her ear. "I can't wait to be inside you," he whispered, then sucked her earlobe.

He cupped her breasts, squeezing, pinching her hard nipples through the silky fabric. As she closed her eyes, the sensations rushed over her. His hard length pressed against her back and her pussy clenched tight, needing one of them, either of them, inside her.

Gryff still stood frozen in the center of the room, his cock appearing harder than it was moments ago. She reached a hand out to him.

One beat. Two beats. Three heartbeats later, he came closer, entwining his fingers with hers. She tugged, encouraging him to join them on the bed. He moved to her front, and with Trey behind her, she was truly sandwiched between them. It felt amazing and made her light-headed at the thought of these two men being hers. All hers.

They were here to pleasure her and only her. Make her feel good. Make her feel beautiful and wanted.

With hands to his face, she pulled Gryff closer, kissing his lips softly. She pulled away before he could deepen the kiss. "Kiss me again, but down there. Make me come with your mouth, Boss. Show me what it's like to lose my mind. To forget everything but you between my thighs."

His eyes hooded and his breath hitched as he stared into her soul.

"Please, Boss."

He looked behind her at Trey. "Pull her back."

Trey helped her maneuver, so she was no longer on her knees, but leaning back against his chest, her head at his collar bone as he leaned against the headboard. His cock felt hard against her.

"Should we take off her dress?" Trey asked.

"No. Leave it for now. She's not wearing panties."

No, she wasn't. She hadn't all night. Now that he settled between her legs and slid the silky fabric up her thighs, it was obvious.

She felt wet, slick, warm. Very ripe for his mouth. He couldn't touch her soon enough with it. She squirmed under Gryff's touch, against Trey's body.

Trey pressed his lips to her ear again. "Shh, baby. He's going to make you come really soon. I'm going to help. I want to watch you come. I want to hear you come. I want you to call out our names. I want you to beg us to fuck you."

"Yes," she murmured. As Gryff slid two fingers between her folds, separating her, she gasped. Then his tongue stroked her, teased her clit. Those long fingers of his slipped deep, his lips sucked at her sensitive nub. Watching his head buried between her thighs just about made her fall apart.

Trey cupped her breasts under the loose fabric of her dress, finding her aching nipples. He pinched each one between thumbs and forefingers, gently twisting back and forth until she cried out, "Harder."

He pressed his cheek into the crook of her neck, whispering words that could drive her to the edge on their own. With his hands on her, the heat of his body against her back, Gryff's mouth on her slick pussy, it didn't take much for her neck to bow, her eyes to squeeze shut, and her hips to surge against Gryff's hand and mouth.

"I'm coming." She wasn't sure if they heard her. Her words were no more than a ragged breath.

"That's it, baby. I bet you taste so good right now," Trey murmured against her ear. "Warm and wet. I might have to taste you next. That was only your first orgasm. There's going to be so many more tonight. I promise."

If they were all as intense as the one she just had, she might not last the night.

When Gryff lifted his head to look at them, his lips glistened with her arousal. Trey said, "Come here. I want to taste you both."

Surprisingly, Gryff complied, pushing himself to his knees and leaning close, squeezing Rayne between them as they kissed over her shoulder. She groaned at the intimacy of the act.

When they both thrust against her at the same time, she just about lost her mind. The thought of Trey taking her from behind and Gryff from the front made her head spin. It was something she definitely wanted to try. Not tonight, though.

Like Trey said, baby steps.

As soon as Gryff broke the kiss, he took her mouth while Trey sank his teeth gently into her shoulder. Her back arched and her nipples pushed into Gryff's chest. With a last sweep of his tongue over her lips, Gryff pulled away and told Trey, "Take that nightie off her."

"It's not a nightie," she murmured, her mind fuzzy with what was about to come.

"From now on it is. You won't wear that out of the house."

She blinked, realizing he wasn't joking. He was serious and normally she would argue. But his demand turned her on even more. "Yes, Boss," she answered.

"Sorry, baby, but I agree with boss man. No one should see you in this little number but us," Trey stated as he drew her arms and the green satin sheath over her head. "On your hands and knees. Face boss man. It's time for dessert."

Gryff kissed her lightly before helping her into the position Trey wanted, which put her at the perfect spot to take Gryff into her mouth. And she did so, wrapping her lips around him, sucking him as deep as she could. His fingers raked through her hair then found purchase. She whimpered around him when Trey's tongue stroked her pussy, his fingers teased her clit. He nuzzled and nipped, making it hard for her to concentrate on Gryff. Though, she heard no complaints. She let his fingers guide her head, back and forth along his length. If she didn't need her hands to hold her weight up, she'd have one wrapped around the root of his cock, the other cupping his soft sac, so she tickled the area where his cock met his sac with her tongue instead. His hips jerked. He must like that. She stored that little tidbit away in her memory for future use.

Figuring out Gryff's likes became quickly forgotten as Trey slipped two fingers inside her. She heard the snap of the lube cap and felt the cool gel drip over her anus. He had done this the other night, too. He had teased her and worked her open until she begged him to slide a finger, then two, into her tight canal. She loved ass play and Trey hadn't been the first to explore that with her. So, when he started to tease her back there again, she moaned around Gryff's cock, her eyes rolling back when Trey pressed a finger past her tight ring. He worked her slowly, two fingers in her pussy, one in her ass until she climaxed around him, tightening her jaw so she wouldn't clamp down on Gryff.

Before the waves of orgasm finished, Trey replaced his fingers with his mouth, sweeping a tongue along her slick folds, tasting her arousal, her climax, while still working her ass.

It was the most glorious thing she ever felt.

"Watching you do that while she has her mouth on me is not helping my endurance," Gryff groaned to Trey.

Trey rose to his knees, pressed closer between her thighs and before Rayne or Gryff realized what he was doing, thrust deep inside her. One hand grabbed her hip, the other still working deep in her ass.

Rayne let Gryff slip from her mouth and pressed her forehead to his lap, lifting her rear higher, moaning against his skin.

"No condom," Gryff growled, his body stiffening.

"Boss, touch me," Rayne cried out, trying to get his attention off the man fucking her from behind. "Touch me."

His dark eyes dropped to hers and it was hard to miss his hard expression, his frown.

"You haven't used one yet," she reminded him, which only deepened his frown. "Really? Right now?" she said impatiently under her breath.

Trey and she had discussed it the other night. However, Gryff had *never* discussed it and now he wanted to pound his chest like a hypocritical gorilla. She wasn't going to have any of that. Especially right now. Especially since his little territorial show had slowed Trey down.

"We discussed it," Rayne said.

"But not with me," Gryff answered.

"No, but then you and I didn't discuss it the first *or* the second time. Before or after. Remember that."

Gryff's jaw tightened for a moment, but she could see his face change as he relented.

Trey had slowed to a stop which did not make Rayne happy. "Are we going to analyze shit right now? Or are we going to fuck?" he asked, sounding a bit peeved.

"We're going to fuck," Rayne answered, giving Gryff a look. Then she gave Trey a smile over her shoulder. "Carry on."

He chuckled, then smacked her ass, making her jump. "I need to get back in the groove, baby."

She wiggled her ass against him playfully. "Spank me again. I like it."

"I know you do, baby. I know you like the sting of my palm

against your ass. Especially when my fingers are deep inside you there, too."

"For fuck's sake," Gryff muttered.

"Gryff, get with the program or get out," Rayne said, giving him a scowl.

"Yeah, boss man, you're bringing me down here," Trey complained. "And I was about to bust a nut."

"*Jesus.*"

"Boss," Rayne warned. "Please. *Please* don't ruin this."

Gryff's nostrils flared over his flattened lips as he searched her face. She didn't hide her displeasure at his attitude. Then he gave a sharp nod and a painful grimace she guessed was supposed to be a comforting smile. Not even close. She rolled her eyes.

He lifted her chin up and met her gaze. "Sorry," he whispered. "This isn't easy for me."

"I understand, but don't— *Oh, fuck!*" she yelled when Trey's hand smacked her ass again, this time even harder. Then she heard a low chuckle behind her. Gryff's eyes flicked to Trey then back to her quickly and she could see him trying to keep his expression neutral.

"You like that?" he asked her, his voice sounding a little more strangled than a moment ago.

He must like that, too.

"Yes," she hissed as Trey slapped her ass again, this time on the other cheek. She looked over her shoulder. "Fuck me while you do that."

"Yes, ma'am," Trey said giving her a grin. He began to move again, his fingers and his cock sliding in and out of her with the same rhythm. She couldn't help but close her eyes for a moment as the sensations overwhelmed her. She opened them when she realized she needed to make sure Gryff felt included. She didn't want to cut him out in any way, even slightly.

"Do something!" she yelled a little too loudly at Gryff.

His eyes widened. "Like stop him?"

"No! Like join in." Her laughter almost pushed Trey out of her.

Then, finally Gryff smiled, his body relaxed a little, and he raked his hands through her hair, made two fists, yanking her head up none-too-gently.

"That's it, Boss," she practically breathed before he took her mouth, sweeping his tongue deep until she pushed back over and over meeting Trey's thrusts. She moaned into Gryff's mouth.

"I'm going to fucking blow," Trey bellowed. "Watching you two kiss... *Ah, fuck*." And with one last hard slap to her rear, he thrust deeply, then pulled out both his cock and fingers as his cum shot all over her ass in long, hot strings. With a groan, his damp forehead pressed against her back as he leaned over her, sucking in air. "Fuck," he groaned.

Not even a second later, Gryff growled, "Get a washcloth and clean up your mess. It's my turn."

With a grunt, Trey slipped off the bed and headed to the master bathroom.

Rayne noticed it wasn't only her watching the quarterback's ass as he walked away from them.

"I can't wait to watch the two of you together," Rayne murmured.

"Right," Gryff answered, swinging his gaze back to her. "Don't hold your breath."

"Right," Rayne echoed, giving him a smirk.

"I'm serious."

"Uh huh."

His lips flattened out, and she struggled to keep from laughing. "I know you want a piece of that. You can fight it all you want, but your eyes give you away." She tilted a head toward his lap. "Not just your eyes."

He grabbed the root of his cock and squeezed. "How do you know this is not all you?"

Rayne's smirk widened into a smile. "Right."

Trey came back with a damp washcloth and gently wiped the evidence of his climax off her skin and gave her another light tap on her rear. "Pretty in pink, baby," he said, indicating the color of her ass cheeks. "Mmm. Can't get enough of a woman who likes a good spanking. How about you, boss man?"

"Right," Gryff echoed Rayne.

Trey tilted his head. "On your back." Rayne shifted to lay on her back, but Trey stopped her. "No, not you. You," Trey said to Gryff. "On your back, boss man. I have an idea."

When Gryff cocked an eyebrow at Trey, Rayne tapped his cheek and said, "Go with it, Boss. Let him direct us. He knows what he's doing."

Since he told her he's had a few threesomes before—and not just threesomes, but more—she trusted him to know what he was doing. She hoped she wasn't wrong.

With a grumble, Gryff spread his large frame on her bed, tucked a pillow under his head, and waited.

"Damn," Trey murmured as he kneeled between Gryff's calves and studied the man laid out before him. "I really want to climb on. But... Oh, fuck... Baby, hop on and face me."

With a last glance at Gryff, Rayne straddled his waist, giving him her back. His hands went to her hips to steady her since his body was wide. She wrapped a hand around his hard-as-a-rock cock and leaned over to quickly lick off the precum that had beaded at the head. His hips jerked slightly beneath her and she heard him blow a breath out behind her.

"When you're ready, baby," Trey encouraged her, giving her his arm to assist her to mount the widest part of Gryff's hips. Both of her knees no longer reached the mattress and her legs were spread so wide she felt a pull in her inner thighs.

Lining Gryff's cock in between her slick folds, she teased him a bit, rubbing the crown back and forth, taking advantage of her own natural lube. She peeked over her shoulder to see Gryff's eyes were dark, his lips pinned together as if he struggled not to thrust up and into her.

With a small smile and Trey's help, she rose then slowly lowered herself until Gryff was balls deep. Sighing and closing her eyes for a moment, she savored the stretch and the feeling of fullness. Gryff's fingers dug harder into the flesh at her hips.

He made a noise that caused her to break out in goosebumps. "If you don't do something soon, you're going to end up on your back," he warned her.

"Patience, boss man," Trey whispered, giving Gryff a look over her shoulder. Then he kissed her, exploring her mouth, moving his lips over hers until she moaned. Trey cupped her breasts and squeezed them together, finally breaking the kiss to drop his head to flick each nipple with his tongue, pluck each hard tip with his lips. His eyes flashed when he said, "Put your hands on my shoulders. Use me for balance."

She did what he suggested and was surprised to see how small her hands looked on his broad, tattooed shoulders. At five-six, she wasn't tiny, but she wasn't large either. Even so, the contrast brought home how big both men really were, not just in height.

Trey leaned closer, nuzzling her neck as Rayne used him to lift and lower herself slowly on Gryff.

"Fuck," Gryff groaned. "Faster."

"No," Trey murmured against her throat. "Go slow. Make this last."

"That's not going to make me last. You're torturing me," Gryff said, jerking his hips.

"Having her hot, wet pussy wrapped around your dick is hardly torture, boss man. Not at all."

"It is when you're trying not to blow your load in thirty seconds flat."

Trey chuckled. "Wait until she comes and those tight muscles of hers squeeze your dick so hard that your brain squeezes, too."

"Shut up, Trey. You're not helping," Gryff grumbled.

Trey chuckled again and pressed his lips to Rayne's shoulder. She figured he was watching Gryff's face as she rode him. When Trey sank his teeth gently into her flesh, she paused mid-motion and gasped.

"Ah, you like that, baby?"

She inhaled a ragged breath. "Do it again."

He did, a little harder this time. She ground her pelvis against Gryff and he bit out a curse.

"Again," Rayne said, her eyelids fluttering closed when Trey moved closer to her neck and then sank his teeth there. "Oh God," she groaned.

"Ah, fuck, baby. Spanking *and* biting. You're my dream girl," he said, dropping his head to her breasts and nipping her there, too.

Her chest heaved, and she rocked her hips, trying to drive Gryff deeper. But it was impossible, he had nowhere else to go. She dropped one hand from Trey's shoulder and found her clit super sensitive to her touch. "Again," she demanded, circling and pressing herself before crying out. "Again, Trey!"

He obliged by sinking his teeth even deeper over her nipple, then tracing the indentations with his tongue.

"Fuck you, Trey. Fuck you. Every time you bite her... Oh fuck. Oh fuck. I can't..."

"Hold on, baby," Trey said. Rayne didn't think he was talking to her. He had called Gryff baby, though he might not have realized it.

His cock became even harder inside her and it throbbed. He was close.

"I want to come at the same time," she begged Trey. "Oh, God. Help me come at the same time."

Without a word, Trey slid backwards to lay on his stomach between Gryff's legs, his face right where their bodies joined. He shifted forward enough to put his mouth to her clit while she was still full of Gryff.

She cried out, her back arching, her hips stilling.

"What..." Gryff started but his words drifted off. "Oh fuck, what..."

Rayne looked down to see Trey's head in between both her thighs and Gryff's, and as he worked her clit with his mouth, she thought, no, *this* was the most glorious thing she's ever felt. Having Trey's mouth on her while Gryff was as deep as he could go...

Her toes curled as she felt the beginnings of a climax. Then Trey dropped his head lower, and he sucked Gryff's sac into his mouth.

"What... the... fuck," came Gryff's breathless complaint.

Rayne dug her hands into Trey's hair as he worked Gryff's balls in and out of his mouth, licking, sucking. One of his long fingers pressed against her clit. He didn't forget about her. Not for a moment.

Such a generous lover. She couldn't be luckier.

Her last thought dissipated as her body rippled around Gryff's length, squeezing him tight. Gryff pulsated hard within her, his body bowing, lifting her up and away from Trey's mouth. Her heart thumped, her body tingled, and her breath was lost for a moment, as the final throes of her climax waned. Within seconds, she became boneless. Trey sat back on his calves and caught her in his arms.

"That's it, baby," he whispered against her temple, brushing her hair out of her face. "That was beautiful. You need a big mirror in here so you can see how you look as you come with him deep inside you."

She tried to shake her head, but it was impossible, so instead she laid her cheek on his shoulder and caught her breath.

She figured she'd move once Gryff softened. But he didn't. Not right away. At least his fingers no longer had a death grip on her hips. Instead, he slowly stroked her back with long, soothing movements. If she was a kitten, she'd be purring.

"You good?" she asked Gryff, wanting to see his face, but still too spent to move.

"Very," he answered, sounding a little out of breath himself.

"You need help?" Trey asked her.

"Yes, please."

He wrapped an arm around her as he helped lift her off Gryff's hips. Before letting her collapse onto the bed, he took her into his arms and kissed her thoroughly. Then he guided her next to Gryff.

"Better?"

"Yes, thank you. I'm not helpless. I'm still in ecstasy."

"I can see that," Trey said, an amused expression on his face. "First me, then big boy here. I'm sure we've tired you out."

"But it's a good tired."

Even though she had a king-sized bed, when Trey snuggled in beside her, it was tight. Trey laid on his side, watching both her and Gryff with a satisfied smile on his face.

"Did you like that?" he asked Gryff.

She wondered if he'd answer honestly. Gryff turned his head toward them, met Rayne's eyes first with a look she didn't recognize and then he met Trey's questioning gaze.

"That was fucking crazy good."

Trey gave Gryff a big smile that lit up his whole face, then leaned over to kiss Rayne on the nose as he stroked her arm. "He thought it was crazy good."

Rayne sighed in relief. "I second that. That is my new favorite position. We'll have to make up a name for that."

"Like the Reverse Cowgirl Chow Wagon."

Gryff snorted and Rayne couldn't help but be thrilled that Gryff was starting to accept Trey's attention. Not to mention, actually admit he liked it.

There was hope yet.

"But I get to cowboy up next."

"Not tonight," Rayne said softly, giving Trey a warning look. He shouldn't push Gryff tonight.

"No, not tonight," Trey agreed, but sighed, looking a little disappointed. "When you're ready, boss man."

"And if I'm never ready?"

Rayne reached out blindly for Gryff's hand and squeezed it. He intertwined their fingers together and raised them to his lips to kiss her knuckles, then he laid them on his chest.

Trey must have been in the same mindset as her. Because neither answered him. Neither wanted to think that far in advance. Nor so negatively. Rayne believed Gryff would come around, would eventually openly accept his desires, it just might take a bit of time.

Time all three of them had... unless Trey ended up in jail for a few months.

Which could very well happen. She frowned.

"No frowning, baby. I'll accept whatever he decides."

Trey mistakenly thought her frown was due to Gryff's question. She'd allow him to continue to believe that. There was no point in bringing up his charges at this moment. She wanted to enjoy being sandwiched between both of them. There was time enough to worry about legal issues during the day.

Gryff rolled onto his side to face Trey. "I haven't said yes. I haven't said no."

"And you don't need to right now," Rayne assured him. "Can we change the subject?"

"Yes, let's. Why did you get the tattoo?" Trey asked him. "I've never seen anyone with such a big piece that only had one. Usually people start small."

Gryff hesitated so long, Rayne didn't think he would ever answer. "I was young and stupid."

Trey shook his head, then propped his head in his hand. He now lazily stroked Rayne from her throat, around her breasts down to her pubis, and back up. "You didn't get that when you were young and stupid."

When Rayne first saw it and asked, she didn't think he got it when he was young, either. The piece was too big. Too expensive. And the work appeared to be quality.

"No, I got it because I *had* been young and stupid."

Trey suddenly leaned in closer as if he didn't want to miss that story. "Young? Stupid? There's no way. I can't picture you, the great Gryffin Ward, like that."

Gryff frowned at him. "It happens."

"Sure. And sometimes you can be stupid when you're not so young."

"You mean like you."

Rayne didn't miss the flash of something—hurt, maybe—in Trey's eyes.

"Yes, like me," Trey finally answered quietly. "I realize I don't rate up there with you, Gryff. Not even close. Yes, I make money because I can throw a damn ball really well. But I'm not good enough for you. I'm an embarrassment, right? Remember when I said I'd be the spot on your spotless reputation?"

Rayne laid quietly, her heart squeezing for Trey, for the hurt in his voice. He truly believed that Gryff wasn't accepting him, not only because Trey was a man, but one with baggage.

Rayne wanted to question Gryff about it. But not now. It was best to let whatever would play out between them to do just that without her interference. At least they were past the point of Gryff wanting to beat Trey's ass. Trey wanted Gryff to accept him as an equal. As a lover.

And Gryff still struggled with it.

"It wasn't always spotless, Trey," Gryff admitted softly.

CHAPTER 9

R ayne looked at Gryff in surprise, but he avoided her eyes, dropping flat on his back again to stare up at the ceiling.

He didn't want to talk about this. Not with Rayne. Not with Trey. Not with Grae. Not with anyone.

He couldn't ignore his past, but he worked hard to get where he was. To be as successful as he was.

There was nothing wrong with being young and stupid. To a point. But he'd bypassed that point and had made some dangerous, possibly life-changing choices.

He didn't necessarily want to forget about them. Hence the tattoo. But he didn't want to flay himself open for others to judge him.

Though, he had judged Trey.

More than once.

Fuck.

Grae was right when he said Gryff had no right to judge.

"I'm sorry."

Trey reached over Rayne and curled his fingers around Gryff's bicep. "For what?"

"For unfairly judging you. I have no right."

Rayne rolled on her side to press against him and Trey spooned her back. She ran her fingertips across Gryff's furrowed brow, trying to smooth it out.

The three of them were not in any type of relationship, conventional or otherwise. He did not need to spill his guts to them. They did not need to know about his deepest, darkest secrets.

They did not.

But for some reason, he wanted to tell them, to get it off his chest. Hell, to get the dragon off his shoulders. For them to understand where he came from, why he was the way he was.

He couldn't explain why he needed to relieve his burden. He just did.

Maybe it was the intimacy they currently shared. Maybe it was the pull he felt tonight once they all bared themselves to each other. Physically and emotionally.

No matter what, something pulled at him and it wasn't just sexual. It wasn't just the physical release.

He turned his head and studied the two of them, who, in turn, quietly studied him.

His chest tightened, and he suddenly got very, very scared.

What the fuck was happening to his life? How did he end up in bed with not only one of his employees but a man, and one who was a client as well?

He blinked.

"Don't you dare pull away from us now," Rayne said, her eyes getting sad. "Boss... Gryff. Please. Don't shut us out."

He closed his eyes, sucking air through his nostrils. His heart suddenly raced, and he was spinning out of control.

He couldn't be having a panic attack. He was stronger than that.

His lungs felt like they were collapsing and he couldn't catch his breath. He desperately reached out for them...

When their hands found him, when their warmth touched his

skin, his chest started to rise and fall smoothly again. His vision cleared. His thoughts stopped spinning.

He blinked, then whispered, *"Jesus."*

Rayne stroked a knuckle down his cheek. Trey squeezed his fingers. Neither said a word. He couldn't look at them, couldn't see the concern in their eyes. He needed to get out the words before he couldn't.

"I came from a great home. Loving, successful parents. My siblings... I had everything. My stars were aligned. All I had to do was graduate, and I was guaranteed a spot at a good college on my parents' dime. I didn't need a scholarship to help me get an education. It waited for me."

"I worshipped my brother. I doted on my sisters. But I got careless. Life became boring, predictable. No challenge. My brother had football, but unlike him, I didn't want to play sports. I didn't want to do much of anything but hang out with my friends. Play video games. Party."

He took a deep breath and closed his eyes, remembering. "One type of party lead to another type. And then suddenly the crowd around you starts to change. People fall out, other people fall in. Maybe not the right people. Maybe not the friends who would've dragged you home before curfew, or who would've looked after you. No. Instead, it became people who encouraged you to party longer, harder. Fuck school. Fuck my parents. Fuck everything but chasing the high. Then, suddenly your life centers around finding that high until that thrill dulls. Then you search for the bigger thrill. For the ultimate high. I started chasing that elusive dragon."

"Gryff..." Rayne whispered.

Gryff raised a hand to stop her words. He needed to get this all off his chest. "I chased that dragon until the dragon caught me. Dragged me down. Then I did something really stupid because my more than generous allowance was no longer enough to sustain me. I got caught. I thought my life was over, but I was lucky. I had parents who stood by me and could afford a great attorney. I got a second chance. I took that opportunity and ran with it, never looking back."

If his father hadn't gotten him a good defense attorney, he would have been convicted and thrown into the system. If he had been thrown into the system, he might not have ever escaped and never made anything of himself. Because of that, he decided to help others out, try to keep the innocent, or the people who made a stupid mistake, out of the endless cycle of the system. Give them their second chance like he was lucky enough to get. He was forever grateful for that attorney.

"I don't chase the dragon anymore. I've slayed the bastard. I carry him on my shoulders as proof and as a reminder. This is why I'm hard on myself." He rolled onto his side and faced both of them. "This is why I'm hard on you, Trey."

Trey had his chin leaning on Rayne's arm and his thigh draped over hers as he listened. When Gryff met his eyes, Trey snaked his arm around his neck, pulling him closer to give him a quick kiss on the lips, then released him.

"I want to be that defense attorney who gives you your second chance. You have a gift. Don't blow it."

"That's why I need you two."

Gryff shook his head. "We'll get you out of this. Then it's up to you to continue down the right path, to stay out of jail, to stop the bar fights, to stop the locker room brawls, the back-alley hookups. If you want to be with me, with *us*, you need to keep your shit together. I won't be able to sit back and watch you crash and burn. I *won't* watch it. Remember that."

"Got it, boss man. I want to keep you two at my back and I want to keep you two in my bed. I promise to keep my shit together."

"And I promise to try to be more flexible when it comes to the three of us being together."

"You mean, when we're doing the nasty? When we're knockin' boots? Rocking the boat? When we're—"

Gryff punched him in the arm.

118

"Ow," Trey complained, rubbing his arm, but shot Gryff a big grin and then laughed.

Rayne shook her head. "You two." She pinned Gryff with her gaze. "Thanks for sharing, Boss."

"No," Gryff murmured, the weight on his chest a little lighter. "Thanks for letting us share you."

CHAPTER 10

From her home to his in a blink. The nights flew by. The days dragged.

Gryff hadn't stayed late at the office in the past two weeks.

Not once.

Neither had Rayne.

The daylight was for others. The nighttime was for them. Only them.

Rayne had been having discussions on a daily basis with Grant Lane, the associate Gryff appointed to "head" Trey's case.

Grant was very good. But not Gryff good. And certainly not even close to Rayne.

But she had countless meetings in the office with Grant. Assisting him with the District Attorney, gathering facts, searching for witnesses. Anything to get Trey's charges dropped. They had even deployed the firm's private investigator, Elliott, who happened to be one of the best in his profession.

Gryff only wanted the best for his firm. That's why he was on top. He didn't slack and none of his people did, either. He had no room or patience for dead weight.

Gryff wasn't billing Trey for all the hours Eli was putting in, though he didn't tell Trey that.

They needed to avoid a trial. If the DA didn't agree to dismiss the charges, then the next step would be to make a deal. Trey balked at that option. Grae also had weighed in on that route. He didn't want a deal either. He wanted Trey completely cleared of any charges.

But, no matter what, they needed to keep Trey out of the clutches of Judge Thompkins.

In the last two weeks, the three of them had gone nowhere together in public. Trey was too recognizable and the media sometimes lurked. Especially the gossip rags.

They avoided his apartment, with most nights ending up at Rayne's or Gryff's. Trey had even rented a plain Jane Honda to travel to and from either place. He'd wear an old, ratty baseball cap, sunglasses, and sometimes a hoodie to avoid attention.

But, even so, there hadn't been one night that the three of them had not been together.

Gryff wasn't stupid. He knew Trey was "grooming" him to become his lover in all ways.

As fun as the last two weeks had been, the late nights had taken a toll on him and Rayne. They'd arrive at work in the morning exhausted, sucking down cup after cup of coffee. They couldn't keep going like this.

Trey? Not so much. Being suspended from the team gave him nowhere to report. He could sleep in, get a massage, lounge around his penthouse, and work out in the middle of the afternoon. Followed by a nap.

A fucking nap.

Even Rayne had rolled her eyes at that confession.

In those two weeks, rules had slowly formed. Not officially. But they were *understood*.

Because of the lack of condom use, Gryff insisted they all get tested and then continue to test on a regular basis for however long this all lasted. No one had balked at that.

The next rule Rayne had insisted on...

She would have whoever, whenever and wherever she wanted. No jealousy allowed.

Gryff wasn't thrilled with that rule. Trey couldn't care less.

But, Trey added, if he wanted to be alone with Gryff, she couldn't gripe. Gryff found it mildly amusing that she agreed, though reluctantly. And not before insisting how hot it was to watch the two of them together.

However, besides kissing, touching, and sucking, nothing more had progressed between Gryff and Trey.

When Trey said he would go slow, he'd meant it. And though Gryff appreciated it, he was now ready to move forward.

He wanted Trey, he knew that now. Seeing the man naked for the past almost fourteen nights had whetted his appetite. Not to mention, the man had mad skills with his mouth.

Tonight, they were meeting at his house. Since it was Friday, he asked them to bring a bag, to stay the night. Something they hadn't done before. At the end of every night, no matter how late, they'd all gone their separate ways.

Tonight, that would change. Trey's smart comment had been, "I thought you'd never ask."

When he told Rayne this morning, her reaction had been, "You got it, Boss." And with a toss of her hair and a knowing smile, she sashayed out of his office in one of those ass-hugging skirts, leaving him with an erection that trapped him behind his desk for a full ten minutes.

Gryff's cell buzzed on his desk. A glance at the lit screen showed a text from Trey.

When you said pack a bag, did that mean pack some toys and a vat of lube?

Before Gryff could answer him. Another text came through: *You have condoms?*

Gryff stared at the phone. Neither of them used condoms with

Rayne. He could only think of one reason for needing condoms. Trey guessed that they were taking it to the next level.

Gryff steepled his fingers in front of his face and blew out a breath.

His phone buzzed again. *You don't know how hard I am thinking about tonight.* And again: *Can you two leave the office early?*

Please?

Okay, fine. Ignore me. I'm going to prepare myself. Because I know I'm playing receiver tonight.

"For fuck's sake," Gryff muttered, a knot forming in his stomach. He thought he was ready... But maybe he wasn't.

It was one thing to fantasize about being with Trey. It would be quite another to actually follow through. He'd woken quite a few nights with a hard-on that wouldn't quit when he had dreams of the two of them together.

It was now or never. Because if it was going to be never, then Trey needed to know that. Then it would be up to the other man to decide if he wanted the three of them to continue as-is or not. It seemed that Rayne wanted all of them to be partners equally. Which meant all of them giving, all of them taking.

Gryff leaned back in his chair and squeezed his eyes shut.

Partners.

In Gryff's opinion, partners also meant some sort of relationship. Like a *real* relationship similar to Grae's with Paige and Connor.

They hadn't discussed anything long term. Gryff had just figured once the newness wore off, all three would go their separate ways.

Or at least Trey would wander on to his next conquest, and leave Rayne and Gryff deciding what existed between just the two of them.

Because, no matter what, Gryff did not want to let Rayne go. Even if the threesome eventually dissolved.

He still considered making her a partner in his firm. And lately, a partner in life. She'd be a strong, intelligent woman to stand by his side.

Fuck.

"Boss."

His eyes popped open. He envisioned a serious, possibly permanent, relationship with the woman that just entered his office. If she would accept him.

She closed his office door behind her and approached his desk with a sober look on her face.

Shit.

"I can't concentrate."

She wasn't the only one.

"Are you sure you're ready for this?" She gave him a look of concern as she rounded his desk. He turned his chair to face her, and she stepped between his open knees, pressing her palm against his cheek.

His heart thumped in his chest at her caring touch. "I have to know."

She tilted her head and studied him. "There's no rush."

"I don't see a point in stringing Trey along if I'll never want to be with him completely."

"I'd like to say he wouldn't mind keeping it the way things are now, but I don't think that's what he wants. I think he'd become dissatisfied in the end."

"I know what he wants."

She nodded. "Yes, you do."

"I know what you want."

She stayed silent for a moment. "Yes, but what I want..." She shook her head. "I just don't want you to be pushed into something you might not be comfortable with."

Instead of answering, Gryff curled a strand of her hair around his finger and then let it unwind on its own.

"I don't want you to do something you'll regret."

"No one is pushing me to do anything. If I do this, then it's because I want to," he assured her.

She perched on his thigh and wrapped her arms around his neck, then nuzzled his throat. "I can't stop thinking about it. I'm so wet right now."

"Are you?" Gryff slipped a hand under her skirt and stroked her stockings at the apex of her thighs. The hot dampness under his fingertips gave him an instant erection. *Again.* "Oh, yes, you are. I'm tempted to take you right now."

"Dani might walk in."

"Yes, she might."

Rayne brought her lips a hair's breadth away from his. "I shouldn't even be sitting on your lap."

"No. You shouldn't."

"Boss, if you keep touching me like that, you might make me come. Even over my stockings. I'm that ready."

"That might be a shame." He stroked faster and harder. Rayne squirmed in his lap and he groaned as her ass bumped his cock.

"*Boss...*"

"Tell me to make you come."

"*Boss...*"

"Tell me."

"Oh... fuck. Boss... make me come. Make me—" She tensed and her hips jerked, her thighs squeezing his hand between them. As she cried out, he crushed his mouth to hers to muffle it. Though, he wanted to cry out himself. He was painfully hard, and he doubted that he would get any relief until tonight.

Surprisingly, he hadn't made a mess in his pants when he watched her face contort as she came.

God, she was so beautiful. Especially when she was in the throes of an orgasm.

He dropped a hand to his erection and rubbed it. Jesus, this was the second time today she'd done this to him.

She broke the kiss when her body stopped twitching and pressed her forehead against his while she panted, trying to get her breath back. "I can't wait to do Reverse Cowgirl Chow Wagon again," she whispered raggedly.

"It might not be tonight."

"No."

"But soon."

"Yes," she agreed. "Very soon." She pushed to her feet and straightened her skirt while heading toward the door.

"Rayne," he called out. She stopped and glanced at him over her shoulder.

He wanted to say something to her about how much she meant to him. But it was too soon. And things were still up in the air.

Now might not be the time.

"Boss?" she asked, cocking an eyebrow.

He shook his head. "Nothing. I'll see you tonight. Please close the door behind you."

"Yes, Boss," she gave him a wink and a smile before letting herself out.

He wanted her. And he would have her. Whether it ended up being in a threesome or just the two of them, she was his.

Rayne's chest tightened, and she wrung her hands as Gryff paced his living room. He was giving her a bad case of anxiety with his nervousness.

"Are you sure you don't want a drink?" she asked, indicating the untouched Jack and Coke that sat on a nearby table.

"No."

Well, damn, if he wasn't going to drink it, she would. She snagged the glass and took a healthy sip, the warmth of the liquor snaking into her belly.

"What time is it? Didn't I say seven?"

"You're wearing a watch," she reminded him.

"What? Oh." He lifted his wrist. "Five after."

"It's Trey. When has he been early for any of our... nights together?"

She was surprised Trey hadn't actually been early for once. Especially since he'd been looking forward to tonight and taking that next step.

He stopped abruptly in front of her, pulled the glass out of her hands and downed the contents before handing her the empty glass back.

The corners of her lips curled up. "You want me to make you another one?"

"No."

That meant yes. She went over to the side bar and mixed him another, making it a little stronger this time. She took a quick sip, then headed in his direction until the doorbell rang.

Both of them froze and their eyes met. Gryff's looked a little larger than normal.

"Are you going to answer the door?"

"Fuck," he murmured, grabbed the fresh drink from her, and downed half of that, too.

"Never mind. I'll answer it." She patted his arm and then headed to the foyer, opening the door to an excited Trey.

"Hey, baby," he rushed in, giving her a big sloppy kiss on the lips before backing up and checking her out. "Damn, you look hot."

Rayne wore stilettos, thigh-high stockings with the seam down the back—because they were Gryff's favorite—and a black leather skirt that barely covered the top of the stockings. She had also dug out a red gauzy blouse that was see-through and wore a lacy black camisole beneath it that emphasized her ample cleavage.

When she let herself into Gryff's house earlier, he had met her in the kitchen, took one look at her, cursed loudly, and then threatened to take her against the wall. She had been quite pleased with his reaction.

"You like it?" she asked Trey, knowing he damn well did.

"Meh."

She threw her head back and laughed.

She sobered quickly when Trey whispered, "How is he?"

"Freaking out."

"Shit. Not good," he murmured.

"No."

"I want this, baby."

"I know. He does, too."

"Where is he?"

"Living room."

"I'm in the living room and I can hear you," Gryff called out.

They looked at each other and both said, "Shit," then laughed.

"C'mon, baby. I love that outfit, but, damn, I can't wait to take it off you, either."

"Maybe I should just watch you two tonight," she said as they entered the living room.

"Not going to happen," Gryff said.

"Hey, boss man, give me a proper hello," Trey said, approaching, pulling the glass out of Gryff's steel grip and handing it to Rayne.

"Fuck you, Trey," Gryff said softly, but let the other man wrap a hand around the back of his head and pull him close.

"You will be. I promise," Trey murmured against Gryff's lips before their mouths sealed together.

Watching them kiss made Rayne not only weak in the knees, but created a rush of warmth and wetness between her thighs. She had skipped the panties tonight. And the longer the kiss went on and the deeper it got, the slicker she got.

No, she wouldn't just be watching tonight. No chance of that. At all.

When Trey's hand went to Gryff's hip, he thrust against him and one of them moaned. She didn't know which one, nor did she care. It sent a wave of electricity through her, either way.

When the men finally parted, Gryff looked a lot more relaxed. His gaze seemed to be a bit unfocused. Trey definitely had skills.

"Did you bring a bag?" Gryff asked Trey, his voice raw, rough.

"Of course. I wouldn't miss an opportunity to curl up between you two all night."

"Wait, who said you'll be in the middle?" Rayne teased.

He gave her a wink. "We'll take turns."

"We shouldn't even be talking about sleeping at this point," Gryff said.

"Who was talking about sleeping?" Trey asked. He turned to Rayne. "Baby, can you get me a beer?"

She hesitated. He'd never made her wait on him before. When he gave her a look, she realized he needed a moment alone with Gryff. She nodded. "Sure, I'll be right back. Actually, why don't your beer and I just wait for you two upstairs?"

"Thanks, baby. You're the best."

Her earlier anxiety now quickly turned into excited anticipation while she grabbed a beer from the kitchen and headed up to Gryff's master bedroom to wait.

CHAPTER 11

Trey stared at the Jack and Coke that Rayne had handed back to Gryff before her departure. "You know, Gryff, we haven't discussed it since when I asked about your tattoo two weeks ago. But..." He rubbed a hand over his forehead, worried about how the man would take his next question. "Should you drink?"

Gryff cocked an eyebrow at him. "Really? Suddenly *you're* going to be the responsible one?"

"I've lived through this before. I don't want to live through it again."

Gryff frowned, his brows furrowing. "What are you talking about? Were you an addict?"

"No. My mother was a drunk."

"You never said anything."

Trey swallowed the lump in his throat. "No. Unlike you, I try to forget my past."

"How bad was it?"

"Bad. My sister and I practically grew up in the local bars. Why they even allowed kids in there, I'll never understand. They were holes in the wall, with sketchy regulars. I doubt those bars cared about any rules or regulations. When you're selling cheap draft or well drinks, you make money on quantity not quality."

"You have a sister?"

"Yeah. She took off at sixteen. I have no idea where she is. I haven't heard from her since. I don't even know if she's alive."

"You can afford to find her."

Yes, at this point in his life, he could afford to hire someone to find her. But... "It's not like I can't easily be found. I'm the quarterback for the Bulldogs, for fuck's sake. If she wanted to contact me, it would be easy. So, I assume she doesn't want to be found."

"What about your dad?"

He shook his head. "He died right after my sister was born. That's why my mother started drinking."

"Damn, I'm sorry. Does Rayne know?"

"I didn't tell her, but somehow your P.I. dug up the info on my mother and gave it to her."

Gryff frowned. "Eli wasn't supposed to dig into your past."

"But he did."

Gryff closed his eyes. "Fuck."

He felt the same way about it. A little disappointed that Rayne had to find out about his past that way. Not that he would hide it from her. Or Gryff. But he would have rather told her when he was ready. He was a bit surprised that Rayne never passed the information on to her boss. And their lover. "Yeah. However, the reason I'm bringing this up is... Once an addict, always an addict. Right?"

"I'm not like your mother. I was never an addict. Yes, I chased the high, and yes, I did stupid shit. But it was that stupid shit that got me caught. And I was caught early enough before I was completely lost. I was more of a chipper than anything."

Trey had no idea what he was talking about.

"Casual user. Not long term. Not an addict. Though, weekends were my downfall. I started partying Friday nights and didn't stop until Monday morning when I was supposed to go to school."

"You were lucky then."

"Yes, and I admit that. Plus, I had parents that cared and noticed. But before they could step in, I got arrested for possession and burglary. Luckily, I hadn't entered the house with the other guys since I was the lookout. And I didn't have a weapon like a couple of the others. Not to mention, it helped that I was a first-time offender and was underage."

"Your stars were aligned."

"I guess so. Let me just say that the whole thing was a smack in the face and a kick in the ass. I don't have an addictive personality, which helped. So yes, I can drink moderately without a problem. Not everyone can."

Trey studied the man before him. Gryff was one of the most upstanding men he knew, along with his brother Grae. His parents had done an excellent job at raising their sons to become men.

Trey guessed that he was a bit lucky, too. Though his upbringing was shit, he could have turned out a lot worse. "If it wasn't for a football coach in junior high that had taken me under his wing, things might have turned out disastrous for me. I could have been chasing my own dragons."

Though, he wouldn't have been as lucky as Gryff. No one would've had his back. Especially a football coach who wasn't a relative. Even he had his limits.

"And to stay in good standing with my coach, I did things—" Things that were in no way legal for an adult to do with a teenage boy.

Gryff visibly stiffened. "What sort of things?"

Trey gave him a look. "Let's just say, no one cared when I spent the weekend, or even school nights, at my coach's house. My mother was just glad to get me out of her hair."

Gryff scrubbed a hand over his hair. "*Jesus.*"

"Our *relationship* lasted throughout junior high until graduation.

And once I got a scholarship to college, I left and never looked back. Never came home during the summer or even on breaks. I never went home ever again." Like his sister, he abandoned his surviving so-called parent.

Then Grae recruited him his junior year in college, but told him he had to finish his degree first. And if he did, he was guaranteed a spot on the team.

The first year, he was third string and never got off the bench. The second year, he was second string and only filled in when necessary or during pre-season games. His third year, the first string QB got injured and Trey stepped in to finish out the season with a good record. And from there... he became not only starting quarterback, but a star player.

Until his current legal mess.

He looked at his attorney and lover. They had both started life in two completely different directions and eventually ended up standing in the same living room. Life was funny like that.

And for that, he was grateful.

He may be fighting for his career, but he had the best backing him. And he had what he considered the best in his bed. Tonight, he would make sure that Gryff followed through and that he not only enjoyed it, but that he would want more.

He wouldn't give Gryff the opportunity to regret his decision. And he wouldn't regret being with Trey. Trey swore to himself that he would not be the spot marring Gryff's reputation. Ever.

"I care about you, boss man. Just so you know." Trey said. "I've told you this already and I'll keep repeating as necessary... Only do what you feel comfortable with. I don't want to wait. But if I need to, I will. Because I know it'll be worth it. But let me just say this... I want you. I want you more than any other man I've been with. And that says a lot that I'm willing to wait. Just know that."

"I know, Trey. But you don't have to wait. Let's go upstairs." And with that, Gryff turned and headed toward the stairs, not even waiting for Trey.

A thrill ran through Trey from his head to his toes. *Holy shit.* The man was really ready. All those baby steps had been worth it.

But it wasn't baby steps he took up the stairs. He took the steps two at a time until he caught up to Gryff, nearly knocking the guy down in his excitement.

∼

G ryff knelt on the bed watching Trey and Rayne kiss, while Trey cupped her breasts, playing with her nipples. He watched Trey make her squirm, make her moan and beg for more.

He was hard. So hard that he couldn't help but stroke himself. Though he admitted it turned him on to watch the two of them together, he still had to fight back the jealousy trying to edge in.

Every instinct he had was to claim the woman as his and his alone. No other man should touch his woman. It was a hard disposition to break. In the nights they'd spent together, he had caught himself tensing, his fingers curling into fists and he had to consciously make the effort to relax, to push past his possessiveness. Hell, his caveman, chest beating, hair pulling, tendencies.

Gryff heard Trey say something, but his mind had wandered and he needed to hear whatever he said again. "What?"

"Tonight, it's all going to be about trains," Trey repeated, not taking his eyes or hands off Rayne.

"What are you talking about?"

"Everything we do will be like a train. Just let me be the conductor. You'll like it. I promise."

Rayne wrapped her arms around Trey's neck, and while meeting Gryff's eyes, sank her teeth into Trey's shoulder. The man's back bowed, and he groaned. "Oh... fuck... me."

Gryff's cock twitched in his palm, and he swirled the bead of precum around the crown.

Trey turned lazy eyes to Gryff. "Tonight, me and you will always be connected. One way or another. You okay with that?"

Gryff wanted to say yes, but his lungs felt empty, his heart pounded, and he still struggled to admit what he wanted.

"Boss?" Rayne prompted.

He nodded his head, still trying to suck oxygen into his lungs.

Trey smiled and asked, "Ready?"

Oh, God, was he ready?

He nodded again.

"Baby, sit against the headboard, knees up, thighs spread. Let me see that pretty pussy of yours."

When Rayne did as told, Gryff could see how wet she was. Her folds were swollen in need, shiny with arousal, ready for one or both of them. When she slipped two fingers inside herself, he groaned and gave his cock a yank. He was ready, too, to be in between her sweet, sweet thighs.

"Open up for us. Let's see it," Trey said. "That's it. Fuck. You look delicious. Right, boss man?"

Gryff swallowed hard. He needed to stop acting like a blithering idiot. "Hell, yes. I want to taste her."

"That's the plan," Trey said, backing away from Rayne's spread legs and making room for Gryff. "On your hands and knees, boss man."

Gryff blinked at his gruff command. He did *not* just—

"Boss, come to me," Rayne begged quietly.

He blinked again and swung his gaze to her. She played with one of her nipples with one hand, while she offered the other to him. His jaw loosened, and his fingers uncurled, and within seconds he was between her thighs, inhaling her female scent, spreading her wide, tasting her sweetness. He took long, lazy strokes with his tongue and her mewing became music to his ears.

"Ass up," Trey said, smacking his hip.

If Trey thought he was going to—

"Ass. Up," Trey repeated, more firmly this time. "Don't worry, if there isn't a condom on my dick, you're safe."

Gryff had to assume his dick wasn't wrapped and reluctantly

lifted to his knees, his ass in the air. Vulnerable. The blood rushed in his ears, but he wanted to concentrate on Rayne. He flicked her clit with his tongue, then sucked it hard, pleased when her hips jumped off the bed.

"That's it, baby. I want to hear you. I want to see you pinch your nipples. Yes, like that. Oh fuck. You like his mouth on you, don't you?"

Then Trey became quiet which made Gryff suspicious, nervous even. When Trey's hands grabbed his thighs, Gryff's heart jumped into his throat. Then Trey's hot mouth encased his sac, his hand squeezed the root of his cock and he stroked. Gryff peeked between his knees and saw Trey on his back, his head between his thighs, his tongue stroking his balls.

Holy fuck.

Fingers pressed between the strip of skin between his balls and his anus.

Holy.

Fuck.

Trey used Gryff's thighs to pull his body farther between them, then took the head of his cock into his mouth.

Gryff groaned into Rayne's pussy, which pulled a groan from her. The harder Trey sucked on him, the faster Gryff licked and sucked Rayne's pink, plump folds. He buried his face deeper and then gasped when a finger teased his hole. Yeah, that hole.

Motherfucker.

Before Gryff could worry about hearing the opening of the lube, Trey raked his teeth over the crown of his cock and then licked the length. He couldn't control the forward thrust of his hips.

"Boss, concentrate on me," Rayne begged, trying to pull his attention away from what Trey was doing. Which was sliding a slick finger up and down his crease, pausing on his tight hole at every pass. Pressing, circling, then—

Oh fuck.

The finger of the star quarterback, whose hands were worth an unknown fortune, broke that virgin plane and pressed deep inside.

That was not supposed to happen tonight.

"Relax," Rayne whispered, wrapping her hands around his head and pulling him tighter against her. "Make me come, boss. I want you to make me come."

He did, too. But... But...

When Trey slipped a second finger in, he scissored them, stretching Gryff. The sensation felt weird, strange, new... not unpleasant. He was tight, most likely because he had tensed, but the more Trey worked him, the harder his dick became, the looser his muscles became, until finally, Gryff could take a breath and appreciate everything that Rayne and Trey were offering him at the moment.

As he sucked Rayne's clit, he slipped two fingers in, fucking her as Trey fucked him.

He felt it coming. He couldn't fight it. His balls got tight, his cock got even harder. He was about to explode. When Trey curled his fingers inside of him and stroked his spot, he curled his and stroked her spot.

Quickly, he pulled his mouth away and shouted as he blasted down Trey's throat. He had no idea what he shouted, he probably sounded like a babbling fool. But right now, he didn't care. He was doing everything he could not to collapse on Trey and smother him.

His arms trembled, his thighs shook, and he growled, "Move."

Trey rolled out and away from him. With a grunt, Gryff collapsed to the bed, all the bones in his body suddenly missing.

Holy fuck.

His cheek laid on Rayne's thigh and he looked up her body to see her face flushed, her eyes liquid, and her mouth parted.

"I'm sorry if you didn't come. I got...distracted."

"That was so fucking hot," she answered softly, sounding breathless. "For the record, yes, I came."

"I came, too, if anyone cares." Trey sprawled across the end of the bed on his back, his belly full of his own cum. He grinned at Gryff. "I think that's the first time I ever came without anyone touching my dick, even myself. That was so awesome."

Gryff shook his head at the excitement in Trey's voice and in his expression.

"I just need a few minutes to recover. Then we're getting back on the train."

A few minutes.

Gryff might need more than that. He may need a damn nap. And a sports drink full of electrolytes.

"Baby?"

"Yeah?"

"Can you get me a washcloth so I don't drip all over Gryff's carpet? I don't think he can move."

She smiled as she extracted herself from beneath Gryff's weight. "That's the second time tonight you've asked me to serve you. Let's not make a habit of it."

"I'll make it worth your while in a little bit. I promise."

She sighed as she went to the master bathroom. Gryff had the strength to move at least his eyes to follow her. If he wasn't so spent, he'd get a hard-on just watching her naked hips rock and roll as she moved.

When she came back into the bedroom with a wet washcloth in hand, she looked at Gryff and laughed. "Damn. You're wrecked."

"I had fingers up my ass while he sucked me dry, as well as my mouth on you. Of course, I'm spent. I'm in my thirties, not my twenties. Hell, when I was eighteen I could've come and kept going strong until I came again. Not any longer."

"I hear that," Trey mumbled. "But don't worry, baby, us manly men will take care of your business shortly. Promise."

She refused to hand him the washcloth, instead taking her time to wipe his skin clean. Trey's eyes closed, and he sighed.

Then the green monster took a little bite out of Gryff again.

He rubbed a hand over his eyes and he turned his face away so he didn't get worked up over something he knew he needed to just let go of.

He rolled off the bed and held his hand out. "I'll take it back to the bathroom." Rayne gave him a questioning look, but handed the washcloth to him. He strode into the bathroom, shutting the door firmly behind him.

He threw the damp cloth into the hamper, then braced himself on the sink, staring into the mirror.

Someone he didn't know looked back at him and blinked. Someone who just had another man's fingers up his ass. Someone who just had another man's mouth on his cock and swallowed his load.

And he fucking liked it.

Gryff dropped his head because he couldn't look at that person anymore and took a shuddered breath.

He closed his eyes, wondering if he could do what Trey wanted. Could he do this? Did he even want to do this?

"Damn it," he muttered.

"Boss?" came the soft voice from the other side of the door.

"Rayne, just give me a minute."

Then he heard nothing else.

He had no idea how long he stood there, a war being fought deep within him. Then the door flew open, Trey latched onto his arm and he jerked hard. Gryff, not expecting it, fell forward but Trey caught him and dragged him farther into the bedroom.

"Stop being a shit. Stop questioning yourself. You're going to fuck me while I fuck Rayne. Do you hear me? And you will like it."

What. The. Fuck.

Gryff ripped his arm out of Trey's grasp. "Fuck you, Trey."

"Yeah. I'm waiting. Do it." Trey jammed both palms against Gryff's chest, making him stumble back. Gryff caught his balance and braced himself for Trey's next onslaught. "Stop being a fucking pussy."

But none came. Trey stood in the center of the bedroom, his fists clenched, his breath rapid and ragged. His eyes flashing in anger.

"Tell me you don't want me. Tell me and I'll leave," his voice no longer held anger, but something else.

Gryff frowned.

"Tell me, Gryff, and I'll leave you alone. I'll stop pushing. I don't want to be where I'm not wanted."

Fuck.

Trey's mom hadn't want him. Her buzz was always more important than her own son. Her own children.

Now he thought Gryff didn't want him, either. He could see that Trey was fighting to keep the hurt from his eyes. But he could see it, recognize it. And he was the one that put it there.

He didn't want to be that person. He didn't mean to be that person. It was his own insecurities that made him keep pushing the other man away.

"Get on the bed," Gryff said, his voice rough, raw. "I want you, Trey. I'll show you just how much."

Trey's expression changed. From disappointment and hurt to relief and a bit of excitement.

"Get on the bed," Gryff repeated.

"The lube... The condoms..."

"Get the fuck on the bed."

"Okay," Trey said softly, his gaze sliding to Rayne, who sat up against the headboard, a worried look on her face. "Do you want me to expla—"

"Shut up, and get on the bed."

"Okay." Trey climbed on the bed and moved closer to Rayne, who cupped his cheek and gave him an encouraging smile. When the two of them kissed, Gryff followed Trey onto the bed. He grabbed Trey's ankles and pulled him down the bed away from Rayne.

"What were your plans?"

Trey looked over his shoulder at Gryff.

"What were your plans?" Gryff asked louder, firmer.

"To fuck Rayne while you fuck me."

Gryff gave a sharp nod and found the lube and condoms waiting on the nightstand. Rayne must have put them there earlier in preparation.

"Then fuck her."

Trey grabbed his semi-hard cock and pulled at it. "But I—"

"Fuck her now."

Then, suddenly both of them were hard. Trey from Gryff's commands. Gryff from anticipation.

He no longer questioned what he would do. He now knew with certainty what he would do. And he wouldn't put it off any longer. "I'm going to fuck your ass, Trey."

"Goddamn," Trey whispered.

"That's what you want, right?"

"Yes."

"You want me to be hard for you? Well, I'm hard. You see this? You're getting all of it. Every inch."

"Yes... I..."

"I don't see you fucking her yet."

Trey scrambled up onto his knees, "Baby, normally I'd give you more foreplay, but I don't think I've got the time. Are you ready?"

"Hell, yes," Rayne answered, sliding down the bed, a giggle slipping from between her lips. "I'm so ready for you."

Trey kissed her hard. "I'll make it up to you another time. I promise."

"Just fuck me," she murmured as he settled between her thighs. "And I promise you won't hear any complaints from me."

"None from me, either. Because in a couple minutes, I will be the luckiest guy in the world."

Trey let out a long sigh as he slid slowly into Rayne. He cupped both of her breasts and kissed the tip of each nipple. Then sucked one of them deep. Rayne's fingers dug into his hair, holding fast, her hips lifting and falling with his.

Gryff watched the two of them, Trey's hips thrusting, Rayne's hips rocking to meet him. He stroked himself as Trey's glutes flexed and tightened with each move. Before he could let his doubts creep over him again, he snagged the lube and a condom off the nightstand and sheathed himself.

"Don't be stingy with that stuff, boss man. You're not small. Just saying."

Gryff didn't answer him, instead popping the top on the tube and smoothing the cool gel over his cock. When he finished, he walked on his knees and settled behind Trey.

Then took a deep breath.

Trey reached around and smacked his own ass cheek. "Right there, big boy. Give it to me like you mean it. A little finger action wouldn't hurt first, though."

"Fuck you, Trey."

"Yeah. Whatever."

Trey stilled when Gryff separated his cheeks and liberally applied the lube, and did as asked, working some in with the tip of his finger.

"Damn. Damn," Trey groaned, suddenly pumping harder into Rayne. "Fuck, it's been too long."

That admission surprised Gryff and made him pause. "How long?"

Trey shook his head.

"How long, Trey?"

"Since the coach."

Fuck. He did not want to hear that. Not now.

"You always top?"

"Yes."

"Trey..." Gryff whispered, now questioning this whole thing once again.

"Just do it. I want you inside me."

Gryff closed his eyes for a second, blew out a breath, then grabbed Trey's hips, positioning the head of his cock against his tight rim. Once he was there, once Trey offered himself, Gryff couldn't resist any longer.

"Oh, God," he whispered, scared and excited at the same time. He pressed forward and Trey opened to him, relaxing his muscles, no longer moving within Rayne. He panted. Gryff felt like panting, too. Instead, he gritted his teeth and carried on, pressing forward, going deeper.

He was tight. Trey was a snug fit and his muscles squeezed him. Trey cursed and shifted, then released a low moan.

Finally, when Gryff was fully seated within the man, he breathed. Trey breathed.

"You okay?" Gryff asked him.

"Yes. Good. I'm good."

Good wasn't the word for how it felt to be inside Trey. A calmness overcame him, like it felt right. This was where he belonged. Not only with Rayne, but with Trey. They were pieces of a puzzle that just simply fit.

Then Trey shifted again and the urge to thrust swelled, so he did. He moved within the man beneath him and as his hips pushed, so did Trey's, making Rayne squirm and cry out. Gryff dug his fingers into Trey's glutes, holding on while he moved, while Trey controlled the pace. Tentatively at first, then faster, harder.

"Are you okay?" Gryff heard Trey ask Rayne. That's when he realized she was bearing the weight of the two of them. He dropped his hands to the bed to hold himself up, to relieve Trey and Rayne of his bulky weight. That gave Trey leeway to move freer, which drove Gryff to the edge of madness.

"Aw, Christ," he groaned, knowing it would take only a few moments before he'd lose it. He'd never fucked anyone so tight before. With a grimace, he tried to keep himself under control, tried to make it last just a little bit longer. He wanted them all to come together.

But, he didn't think it was possible. He was at his breaking point. When Trey slammed against him once, twice... the third time, Trey cried out that he was coming. Gryff wanted to thank any deity listening.

He tried to say Rayne's name, but it came out strangled.

"Baby, tell him you're coming. He needs to hear it."

"Gryff," was all she cried out before his vision blurred, his mind spun, his balls drew tight, and he grunted as he came hard. Then came some more, especially when Trey reached around and squeezed his sac, milking every last drop from him. His dick throbbed and Trey's canal hugged him even tighter.

The only sound for a few moments was heavy breathing, and a long satisfied sigh from Rayne who was trapped under Trey's collapsed body, though it didn't look like she minded.

A smile curled Gryff's lips as their eyes met over Trey's shoulder and she smiled back. Then he leaned over and kissed her thoroughly, sweeping his tongue over her lips and into her mouth. When he pulled away slightly, she brushed a bead of sweat off his forehead.

"That was crazy," she whispered.

"I was never into trains as a kid. Now, I appreciate them," Gryff mumbled. "Are you being crushed?"

"A little."

Gryff hooked an arm around Trey's waist and twisted the both of them up and off of her, onto their sides, but still keeping them locked together. He didn't rush to take his arm away. In fact, he tightened it around the man, bringing him closer.

"Better?" he asked her.

"I don't mind the weight of one of you. Both is a bit much."

"I didn't know you liked to spoon, boss man." Trey ran his fingers along the arm that kept him tight against Gryff.

Gryff shifted his hips slightly to remind Trey whose dick was in whose ass. "Do you want me to let you go?"

"No, but I'd rather snuggle after we all clean up. Should we draw straws to see who gets the middle?"

CHAPTER 12

Rayne, curled up on her side, had her bare back tucked against Trey, who had an arm wrapped around her, while Gryff sandwiched his long body against Trey's equally long one. Three peas in a pod, Gryff thought.

Rayne's breath sounded soft and steady as she slept. Trey had snored softly for a little while, too. But now both men were awake, Gryff wasn't sure if he even slept for a minute.

His mind had been too busy reliving the previous night. Which was why his morning wood was practically jammed in between Trey's ass cheeks.

"If you wiggle one more time, you might get this without any lube. Take that as your only warning."

Trey's body vibrated as he chuckled softly, trying not to wake Rayne. At least one of them slept well.

He thought about what Trey said last night. "Has it really been since the coach?"

Trey sighed and carefully shifted onto his back to look up at Gryff. "You mean being topped?"

"You know what I mean."

"Yes."

"Why?"

Trey raised an eyebrow at him before tucking a pillow under his head so he could see Gryff more eye to eye. He lifted a shoulder. "It just worked out that way. I prefer to be the top."

"But you allowed me—"

"Yes. I knew you wouldn't allow it to be the other way around... at least for the first time."

"Possibly every time."

Trey smirked. "We'll see."

Gryff narrowed his eyes and smiled. "Yes, we will."

Trey lifted his head and pressed their lips together lightly.

"That's it? That's all I get after that great ass reaming I gave you last night?"

Trey laughed. "If we start making out, Rayne will wake up and this will turn into a full-fledged fuck session. I'm not sure if my ass can take it so soon this morning."

"Wow. What a wimp."

"Right. We'll see what a man you are after I fuck you in the ass."

Gryff bit his lip to keep from laughing, then sobered. "I need to ask you something."

"What, boss man?"

"This coach... Did he force you?"

"No. I was willing."

Gryff shook his head. "You were a kid."

Trey shrugged as if it was no big deal. "I gave him something he wanted, needed, and, in return, he gave me what I needed. He gave me a future. He's the only person who ever showed me any kind of attention or affection. He made me feel good, Gryff."

"You were a kid," Gryff repeated, slower and angrier this time. "You shouldn't have been making those decisions. Is your mother still alive?"

"No."

"Good. Because I might kill her if she was."

"The alcohol took care of it for you."

"What was the name of the coach." Gryff didn't ask, he demanded.

Trey pushed himself up to sit. "No. No, you're not going to do something stupid."

"I didn't say I was."

"Bullshit. And don't sic your P.I. on him either."

Gryff kept his mouth shut. The urge to find this coach who may have taken advantage of other teenage boys besides Trey washed over him like a rogue wave.

"Gryff, don't even think about it. He's long retired, and he may not even be alive anymore."

"Good."

"If it wasn't for him, Gryff, I'd never have gotten into football. I might have ended up a drunk like my mother. He got me on a good, successful path. I appreciate what he did."

"Fuck. It's still not right."

"Maybe not."

"No maybes about it."

Trey sighed. "Okay. I'm not going to argue about it. But let me just say this… I'm touched that you care."

Gryff blinked. He did care. He felt bad that a teenage boy would have to resort to sleeping with an adult male to deal with surviving. And that teenage boy was Trey. And Trey was… his.

His.

Fuck.

Fuck.

Fuck.

"You okay?"

No. "Yes. Fine."

"You sure? Because you looked a little panicked there for a moment."

Gryff flopped onto his back and covered his eyes with his hand. Trey rolled onto his side and pressed against him.

"Uh, you sure you're okay?"

"Trey…" Gryff whispered.

149

"Yeah, boss man?"

"I, uh—"

"Gryff!" a female voice yelled from downstairs.

Oh shit.

He jackknifed up and scrambled out of bed quickly, grabbing the closest pair of jeans he could find. He gave up trying to pull them on when they wouldn't budge past his thighs.

"Shit. These are yours," he growled at Trey. "Where the fuck are my pants?"

"Gryff! Where are you?"

The whirlwind that was his youngest sister, Gia, was getting closer, causing Gryff's heart to rap like a beat-boxer. He shot a look toward the bed and the two people who just stared at him. One wearing an amused smile, the other, who blinked at him with sleepy eyes, not so much.

"Will you two move?" he asked in panic, giving up the search for his pants and pulling on a pair of long shorts he grabbed from one of his drawers instead.

"Gryff?"

He threw the wrinkled sheet over Trey and Rayne just as his bedroom door burst open and Gia stood frozen in the doorway. One second with a shocked look on her face, the next her eyes narrowed, her expression curious. "Um... Am I in the wrong house? I swear I drove to my brother Gryff's house and not my big brother Grae's."

She tilted her head and pinned Trey with a stare. Her mouth made a quick O before whispering, "Damn. You look familiar. And I know it's not because you've been naked in *my* bed." She shook her head and pouted. "What a shame."

"Gia," Gryff warned.

"So, um..." She waved a hand toward the bed, stepping closer. "You want to explain this?"

"No."

"Hi," Gia said to Rayne. "Wait. She looks familiar, too. Doesn't she work for you?"

"Gia," Gryff growled, grabbing his sister by the upper arm and pushing her toward the door.

She yanked her arm out of his grasp and moved closer to Rayne, her dark eyes wide as she tapped her finger against her bottom lip. "Yeah. I've seen you before. What's your name?"

Rayne slipped a bare arm from under the sheet and held out a hand to Gia. "Rayne Jordan."

Gia accepted it, giving it a firm shake. "Rayne. That's different. I'd ask if you and my brother are tight, but I can figure that out on my own." She smiled and tapped her temple. "I'm smart like that."

"Gia, do you mind? This is my *bedroom*," he growled, his patience dropping from zero to sub-zero.

"No shit. I see the bed. I see these two people in your bed. Oh wait." She pinned her gaze on Trey. "I know who you are. Trey Holloway. You're on my brother's team."

"Gia, why don't you go downstairs and wait for me?"

"Oh, no. Nuh-uh. Nuh-nuh-uh. I'm fine right where I'm at." She waved a hand toward the bed again. "Does this shit run in the family? Did Mom and Dad have another man in their bed that I didn't know about? Am I going to end up as the filling in a two-man sandwich?"

"Would you like to be?" Trey asked. Gryff shot him a frown. The man was finding this all amusing. Gryff was not.

"I don't know. I mean I have an open mind and all. I might give it a go."

"Oh, for fuck's sake," Gryff groaned, pinching the bridge of his nose. Then he gave his sister a scowl and an order. "Get out, Gia. Go downstairs. Now."

But instead, she gasped and circled Gryff, her eyes wide. "What is that on your back and shoulders?" When she finished circling him, she stopped, hands on her hips and looked up at him. "Who are you? And what did you do with Gryffin Ward, my stuffy-assed brother?"

He pointed a finger toward the door. "Get out, Gia. Get out now. I'm serious."

She bounced on her toes as if deciding what to do and then

pouted. "You suck." With that she flounced out the door, slamming it behind her.

"I like her," Trey said, chuckling. "She's got spunk."

Gryff pinned him with a stare. "Don't get any ideas," he warned.

Trey raised his hands up in surrender, the sheet falling low on his hips. "No problem, boss man."

Gryff grimaced. He had let Trey call him that, but he wasn't so sure he liked it. Especially now that he was super cranky. When Rayne called him Boss, it turned him on, but Trey said it more like a smart ass. At least he wasn't calling Gryff "baby" like he did Rayne.

"That reminds me, we need to discuss your nickname for me. But right now, I need to get rid of my sister."

"When you return, could you bring up breakfast?" Trey asked, his eyes crinkled in amusement, his lips twitching.

"I can make breakfast while you deal with Gia," Rayne announced, shoving the sheet off and climbing out of bed.

Gryff lost his train of thought and his breath for a moment as she walked over to his dresser and pulled open drawers, searching for something.

"I just need one of your T-shirts or something."

"Didn't you bring a change of clothes?" he asked.

"Yes, but I don't want to get dressed just yet. However, I don't want to make breakfast while naked either."

Gryff sighed. "Yes, thank you for that. My sister is already going to be running her mouth to the rest of the family. I don't need her taking photos of you naked in my kitchen as proof and posting it on her social media." He pressed past her, dug through the drawer she just opened and handed her a worn T he normally wore to workout.

She slipped it over her head, releasing her long, mussed hair from the neck of the shirt and dragged her fingers through it. It didn't look any different when she was done. Her lips still appeared a little swollen from last night, her eyes soft, and her face relaxed. Even in his oversized T-shirt, she flipped his switch. His cock agreed.

He groaned in misery because he did not want to deal with his sister while sporting an erection. And if he watched Rayne putting around his kitchen frying up bacon, knowing she wasn't wearing any panties under the T, he may very well end up doing that.

"You don't have to make breakfast. I can have something delivered."

She frowned. "No. I can do it. Breakfast is easy. Eggs, bacon, toast. Coffee. See? Simple. You have all that in your fridge, right?"

Ah, Christ. "Yes."

"That settles it. Wanna help?" she asked Trey over her shoulder.

"Should I wear one of his T-shirts without any underwear, too?" he joked.

"Yes, please," Rayne said with a laugh at the same time Gryff shouted, "No!"

"I still want to wear one of his T-shirts, though. It'll be like wearing a Gryff hug all morning," Trey announced.

"Both of you put on a pair of shorts, too," Gryff said, rushing out of the bedroom door before he had a damn heart attack. "Or at least underwear, please."

"Is that an order?" Trey asked.

"Yes," he yelled back towards the bedroom.

"He's no fun," was the last thing he heard before jogging down the stairs to deal with his pain-in-the-ass sister.

Rayne glanced around the table. All three of them wore one of Gryff's T-shirts in various colors. The only odd person out was Gryff's sister, Gia, who had insisted on staying for breakfast, and now her mouth was running a mile a minute.

At least she had helped Rayne with breakfast. As did Trey. Gryff just spent that time trying to hold on to his patience.

His sister was a firecracker for sure. Wicked smart but a bit flighty for her age. Gorgeous, though, and a lot taller than Rayne.

Their parents had given their offspring a great combination of genes. No doubt.

She had lost track of what the younger woman was talking about. Trey seemed to be the only one paying attention anymore. Gryff just stared at Rayne from across the table. Which was kind of disturbing on one hand, flattering on the other.

She wondered if he was imagining the same thing she was... What it would be like to wake up every morning and enjoy breakfast together.

Though, she thought Gryff would enjoy it a lot more if his sister hadn't barged in.

She peeked at Trey. His eyes would bounce from her, to Gryff, and then back to Gia to give her an encouraging smile before trying to get a word in every couple of minutes.

The amusement on Trey's face was clear, though.

Rayne realized Gia was blathering on about football, which surprised her. The woman sounded quite knowledgeable.

However, she didn't miss how many times Gia touched Trey while she talked. The next time she did it, Gryff cleared his throat loudly, drawing their attention. All heads spun his direction.

Gia stopped talking mid-sentence, frowning at her brother. "Something wrong?"

"Can you talk and not touch, please?"

Her eyebrows lifted. "I don't think Trey minds." She glanced at Trey. "Right?"

"I don't mind," Trey answered, smirking.

Gryff sighed and pushed his plate away. "Well, I do, Gia. I mind. So, please do not touch him."

Her jaw dropped then snapped shut. "Jeez. You're just like Grae!"

"Yeah, I remember how handsy you were when you met Connor. Grae didn't like it, either."

"How is it that my brothers attract hotter men than I do?"

"It's a gift," Gryff said dryly.

Rayne dropped her gaze to her empty plate and fought back the laughter that wanted to bubble up.

"Let me just say, holiday meals will be interesting at Mom and Dad's, that's for sure. I mean you and Grae are making up for Gayle and me being single."

Rayne peeked at Gryff at Gia's mention of holidays at their parents. She didn't miss Trey's pointed gaze directed at him either.

"No one is talking about bringing anyone home to Mom and Dad. So, let's drop it."

"So, this is just a fling?"

Gryff's face changed. Then his expression quickly became an unreadable mask. "Gia, we're done discussing this."

"No boyfriend, Gia?" Rayne asked softly, trying to relieve the tension and change the subject.

"No. Apparently, I'm doing it wrong."

"You're young. You have plenty of time."

"You're not much older than me," Gia reminded her.

That was true. But the other woman seemed a bit more immature than her. Not as established in her life and career as Rayne was.

"Is there some secret website somewhere where you find these threesomes?"

"Oh, for fuck's sake," Gryff grumbled and pushed his chair back, standing.

"If you want, I can hook you up with a couple of my teammates, I'm sure—"

"Trey," Gryff growled. "You are not hooking my sister up with anyone."

"But why?" she whined. "Why do you and Grae get to have all the fun?"

"If I remember correctly, you had problems with one boyfriend. Forget two."

Trey decided to be helpful. "Oh, I doubt they'd want to stick around to be boyf—"

"Trey," Rayne whispered. "Seriously, stop poking the bear."

Trey just shot her a look and continued on his dangerous course. "Who said it has to be two guys? It could easily be you with another woman and a man. Right?"

Gia wrinkled her nose up. "I don't—"

"Enough!" Gryff shouted. "Holy shit, I'm going to have a damn aneurism. Time for you to go, Gia. Rayne, can you walk her to her car? Trey and I will clean up."

Rayne's eyebrows shot up to her hairline. They would clean up? Well, she wouldn't question that. She pushed away from the table. "I'll walk you out, Gia."

"But I'm not ready to go," she said with a pout.

"I'll call you tomorrow," Gryff assured her.

"You're so damn stubborn," she whined.

"Yes, I am." He gave her a pointed look. "It runs in the family."

At his sister's noise of disgust, Rayne hooked her hand around Gia's arm and escorted her out of the kitchen.

Trey looked up at Gryff. "You didn't have to be like that. We were just playing."

"You think she's playing, but she's not. She's serious. She's like a dog with a bone. She gets something in her mind and she doesn't let it go."

"You think she'll go home and search for possible dating sites that are for multiple hookups?"

"I don't doubt it."

Trey snorted.

"Not funny."

"You can't be a hypocrite."

"With my sisters, I can."

"That's precious, boss man, that you're so protective."

"Grae and I are the oldest. Gayle came next, then Gia. So, yeah, we tend to watch out for our little sisters."

"She's old enough to take care of herself," Trey murmured, pushing himself to his feet and coming around the table to close in on Gryff.

"Gayle, yes. Gia, not so much."

"Can't wait to meet Gayle."

Gryff pinned his dark eyes on him as he stepped even closer. "I doubt you'll ever meet her."

Trey pursed his lips and narrowed his eyes. "Why? You won't bring us home to your parents?"

Though he half joked, the thought Gryff only wanted them in his bed and not his life bothered him.

No. Not them. Him. Rayne, he'd have no problem bringing home to mommy and daddy.

"Would they have a problem with me being at your side?"

Gryff stacked some dirty plates and headed toward the kitchen. "No."

Trey did the same and followed on his heels. "I don't believe you."

Gryff dumped the dishes into the sink and turned to face Trey. He took the dishes Trey carried and slid them onto the counter.

"They're used to Grae's relationship, right?"

"Yes. The keyword is relationship, though."

Trey jerked his chin up and then tilted his head to study the man before him. The man he let top him last night. He never would have done it if he only thought this was a quick fling.

"You never answered your sister on whether this is a fling or not."

"No, I didn't."

"Is it?"

"What do you want from me, Trey?"

"The truth."

"Why? Since when are you looking for more than a hookup in the back alley of a bar?"

Trey's chest squeezed tight. "Ouch. That hurt."

Gryff's nostrils flared as he leveled his gaze at him. "Have you ever been in a relationship?"

"A serious one? Not really. Most of my partners have been off and on."

"More off than on?"

"I travel for football. It's hard to maintain a relationship. I didn't want to be tied down, anyway."

"But you want to be tied down now?"

Trey hesitated. Did he want to be tied down? Is that why Gryff possibly seeing this only as a fling bothered him so much? "I don't know," he finally admitted.

"I don't know, either, Trey. I'm not ready to make plans to fly out to my parents' place in Arizona with my two lovers because this is all too new."

Gryff was right. It was too new. But, Trey knew what he felt. Or at least, he thought he did.

No matter what, Gryff couldn't deny the connection between the three of them. Trey couldn't either. Conventional or not.

"You'd consider taking Rayne out there for Christmas, though, wouldn't you." He didn't express it as a question because it wasn't. Trey was pretty sure he knew the answer.

"Maybe."

"No maybes about it."

"It's different."

"No, boss man, it's not different. If your parents have no problem with Grae's current relationship with another couple, a married one at that, then they wouldn't have a problem with yours. *Do* they have a problem with it?"

"Not that I'm aware of."

Trey nodded, then stepped between Gryff's spread legs as the man leaned back against the counter. "Well, then..." He curled his fingers around Gryff's bulky biceps and came chest to chest with him. "Then it's you who would have the problem."

Gryff stared at Trey's lips, then lifted his gaze to meet Trey's. "You need to stop calling me 'boss man,'" he murmured.

Trey leaned in. "Why?"

"I don't like it."

"You like it."

"I don't, Trey."

Trey pressed his lips to Gryff's and whispered. "The fuck you don't... *boss man*." With that, he slipped his tongue between the other man's lips while crushing their mouths together.

Trey felt Gryff's deep groan vibrate through his chest. Yes, a connection existed that they couldn't deny.

None of them.

"I see now why you wanted me to take your sister outside. You two just wanted some alone time."

They broke the kiss, both swinging their gazes to where Rayne stood, hands on hips in fake outrage.

Trey stretched an arm out to her and she moved closer until he snaked it around her waist, pulling her tight against the two of them. "I was just getting him warmed up." He took her hand in his and pressed it to Gryff's groin. "See? Big boy is ready for brunch."

"I see that," Rayne said with a smile, her eyes darkening.

"You going to help me take care of his needs?"

"I can do my very best."

Trey laughed, snagged Gryff's hand in one of his, Rayne's in another, and dragged the two of them upstairs.

CHAPTER 13

The three of them sat at a table once again. Though, this time it wasn't the breakfast table. No. This one was a lot larger, less pleasant, and too many people sat around it for Gryff's liking. Five of them on one side: Gryff, Trey, Rayne, Eli, their P.I., and one of Gryff's senior associates, Grant. Then, there were all the others across from them. An ADA, a transcriber, and some other various people in conservative suits and skirts.

Gryff pulled at the knot in his tie and cleared his throat. "Let's cut the bullshit, Charlie. You know and I know that this was a clear case of self-defense. We found not only one witness, but two that confirmed it. If you were smart, you'd dismiss the charges."

Charlie Duncan, Assistant District Attorney, placed his palms on the table and leaned forward. "Ward, are you saying I'm not smart?"

"I'm not saying that, but I can't help it if you take it as such."

Under the table, Rayne slid a hand over Gryff's thigh and squeezed.

"We've got the two witness statements here," she said. With her free hand, she slid the folder across the table toward the ADA. "We can bring them in for a deposition, if necessary."

Duncan's eyes narrowed as he glanced from the folder that sat in the middle of the table to Gryff. "I'm surprised you're taking a personal interest in Holloway's case."

Gryff kept his expression neutral. "I always take an interest in gross injustice."

"Gross injustice," Duncan repeated and then barked out a laugh. "Do I need to show you the pictures of the guys he put in the hospital?"

"I've seen them."

"He had every right to protect himself," Rayne added. Her fingers tightened on his thigh. Probably more to calm herself than him now.

"He did more than protect himself," Duncan reminded them.

"He was being jumped by four men. I'd say he did what was necessary to survive," Gryff replied, low and slow, so there was no mistaking his words.

"The officers on scene didn't think so. Nor did the DA." Duncan shot a look toward Trey. "He's lucky they didn't tack on sexual assault in addition to the agg assault."

Trey stiffened. "That guy wanted it."

Out of the corner of his eye, he noticed Trey's head spin toward Rayne. She was probably now squeezing his thigh, too, trying to keep him quiet and under control.

Duncan's eyes cut to Trey and studied him. "Are you saying you're gay, Mr. Holloway?"

"He's not saying anything," Gryff answered before Trey could. "And even if he was, it's no one's business."

"Except the guy he tried to sexually assault."

Gryff closed his eyes for a moment and inhaled a deep breath through his nostrils. He tamped down his growing temper.

"If you believed he tried to sexually assault the *gentleman*, why wasn't he charged with that?"

Why not? Because they all knew it was bullshit, and the aggravated assault was easier to prove since physical evidence existed. That's why they charged him with what they did. But Duncan would not admit that.

No, he certainly wouldn't.

Duncan steepled his fingers and leaned back in his overstuffed, overpriced chair, one of many that surrounded the long table. "So, let's deal."

Gryff pinned Duncan with a stare and said, "Let's."

"We're willing to drop the felony charges to two misdemeanor assaults. This way he only does maybe six months or so if he's a good boy. Plus, he pays a fine and their medical bills. It's better than the year or two he might get if convicted of the felonies."

Gryff pursed his lips pretending as if he actually contemplated that ridiculous offer. Though, he would never consider it. No way did he want Trey doing any jail time. Or taking a plea. His career with the Bulldogs would be over. Another team may pick him up eventually, but that was no guarantee. "No."

Duncan didn't look surprised. He heard a relieved sigh from Trey's direction down the table. He ignored it.

"Okay, I get you want to play hardball. I'm willing to give a little bit. How about this? He pays the medical bills for the two men who ended up in the hospital. And he pleads to two counts of simple assault. He may do three months or so. He'll be in and out before anyone misses him."

"You insult me and my client," he murmured, not breaking Duncan's gaze.

"Ward, really. That's a good deal. You should jump on it."

"No."

"Okay..." Duncan blew out a breath, leaned over to one of the suits that flanked him and they talked low to each other. When he straightened, he said, "He just pays for all the victims' medical bills. And any future bills that stem from this assault."

Victims. Assault. Gryff's jaw tightened. His teeth started to grind, but he stopped them. He needed to keep his temper under control. This is why you don't represent someone you have personal involvement with. Emotions become tangled and it gets messy.

Trey jumped in when Gryff didn't answer right away. "Yeah, I can—"

Gryff shot him a look and Trey immediately shut up, lifting his hands slightly off the table in a half-assed show of surrender. Gryff had warned him before the meeting to keep his mouth shut unless Rayne or Gryff, or even Grant, addressed him.

"No."

Duncan's eyebrows spiked. "That's my best deal."

"I doubt it. You're an ADA, what do you care about medical bills?"

"Just trying to get justice for the victims."

"Justice." Gryff snorted. "Right. The whole issue is that they got what they deserved. They weren't victims. My client was the victim. You keep ignoring that fact."

"Let me say this… Thompkins is chomping at the bit to preside over this trial. He hopes there's no deal."

"Why? That doesn't sound like impartiality to me."

"Why ask why when it comes to Thompkins? We all know he's a bastard. He'd probably get a kick out of sending your boy to jail."

Your boy.

If Duncan only knew how much Trey was actually *his boy.*

"So, half their expenses then." At Gryff's hesitation, Duncan sighed and rubbed a hand over his eyes. "Come on. I've got better cases to deal with. Bigger fish to fry. I don't want to waste my time on a trial in this case, either. Work with me here."

"No."

"Jesus, Ward. What the hell do you want from me?"

"What I've been clear about from the beginning. A complete dismissal of charges."

"You're crazy. You said yourself, you've seen the photos of their injuries."

"Yes." Gryff stood up, sliding the untouched folder that still sat in the center of the table to directly in front of Duncan, and said, "I'll give you time to read the witness accounts. Fifteen minutes should do it."

Then he spun on his heels and left the conference room. His gaze sliced through Trey, Eli, and Grant as they scrambled to get out of their seats to follow him. Eventually, Rayne followed, shutting the conference room door firmly behind her.

He ignored the sparkle in her eyes and the pleased look on her face, and kept walking until he hit the glass double doors in the lobby and he stepped into the sunlight, sucking in fresh oxygen. Or somewhat fresh oxygen, since they were in the city and mid-day traffic filled the air with exhaust fumes. He studied the cars all trying to get somewhere fast, but getting snarled in traffic instead.

Grant stepped to his side. "Why are Eli and I here? You seem to have things under control."

"I'm beginning to wonder that myself." His voice sounded a little harsher than it should be so he softened it before saying, "Why don't you two head back to the office? They will dismiss the charges."

Trey squeezed between Grant and Gryff, bumping into Gryff's side. Gryff curled his fingers, resisting the urge to touch him. It wouldn't do to be standing on steps of the downtown District Attorney's office, clinging to his male lover.

"What?" Trey's fingers brushed against his. Just slightly and only knuckle to knuckle. Nothing too obvious. "How do you know?"

Their gazes locked. "I know."

Grant whacked Trey on the back and said, "This is why he's the best, Holloway. Right, Eli?" He looked up at the black P.I. who was just as large, if not larger than Gryff.

"He certainly is," Eli confirmed.

Then, with Eli by his side, Grant walked away, shaking his head with a smile.

Trey spun and gave a questioning look to Rayne, who only shrugged and wandered over to a nearby low concrete wall to perch on it. She lifted her face to the warmth of the sun.

Suddenly, Gryff's gut twisted as he watched her take a deep cleansing breath and close her eyes, her face still upturned. The sunlight made her hair glow around her. Her lips parted and slightly curved at the corners.

The shoes she wore had to have three or four inch heels and made her legs look endless, especially in those damn stockings of hers. Her skirt rode up slightly and he wondered if the stockings were thigh-highs. He couldn't imagine her wearing anything else. He had the feeling the traffic would become more snarled if drivers caught a glimpse of her basking in the sun. She may even cause some rear-end collisions.

A whisper came close to his ear, "Stunning, right?"

Just then Rayne turned her head toward them, saw them standing close together, and gave them a warm smile. One that turned his blood to lava as it flowed through his body and landed in his balls.

He realized it wasn't just a sexual reaction. No, it was more.

He wanted more.

Not just now. Or later. Or even tomorrow.

He wanted forever.

And that thought hit him hard. So hard his knees almost buckled, his heart raced, and a bead of sweat popped out on his forehead. He swiped it away with a shaky hand.

"You don't look so well," Trey observed.

"I'm fine." *Just a little shaken.*

He finally peeled his eyes from Rayne and plastered them on the man standing next to him.

Trey should be considered competition.

But he wasn't.

He shouldn't be attracted to Trey. Not with a beautiful feminine specimen like Rayne only feet away.

But he was.

He shouldn't be wondering when the next time Trey and he would be naked, exploring each other, satisfying each other's needs.

He shouldn't, because all he had to do is suggest getting together and both of his lovers would be willing. More than willing.

Trey did not have to steal moments in the back alleys of bars. Not any longer, at least.

No. He had woven himself into their lives. Made them want him. Made them care.

Gryff thought about the decision that was being made inside that conference room at that very minute.

They might lose Trey either way. Either he'd go to trial and he may end up in jail, which would pull him away from them for a time. Or the charges would be dismissed and the team would take him back, which in effect would put Trey back on the road for training, preseason, regular season. Not to mention everything else that went with being a star quarterback. That would actually last a lot longer than the jail sentence he would be handed if found guilty of aggravated assault.

No matter what, Trey didn't deserve the hand he'd been dealt in this case. He needed to be completely exonerated.

Gryff wouldn't accept anything less. His lover needed a clean slate. And he was the one that could give it to him.

Gryff's long legs were cramped in the back of the cab. Being alone in the back seat, he twisted enough to stretch his legs a little more. Trey and Rayne had taken another cab together since they planned to go celebrate.

Even though Gryff was just as relieved as them, he didn't feel in the mood to celebrate with them. He had other things on his mind.

When his phone chirped, he figured it had to be Rayne or Trey begging him once more to come join them.

He looked at the screen. Grae.

Well?

Gryff responded. *Charges dropped. File closed.*

Possible civil suit? Grae asked.

Doubt it. Those witness statements were solid gold. If so, we'll deal with it.

There was a long pause before he got another text from Grae. With the length of it, Gryff realized why.

The Bulldogs' owners will be pleased. He might not be ready in time for preseason, but he'll definitely be ready for September, then the journey to Super Bowl Sunday. At least he'll be out of your hair now.

Gryff read the last sentence again. *He'll be out of your hair now.*

That reminded him of the conversation at his older brother's home where Grae stated he didn't want to sit across from Trey at the Thanksgiving table and see him eating their mother's sweet potato pie.

It must have reminded Grae, too. *Now it's guaranteed he won't be at Thanksgiving dinner. Game in Seattle that day.*

Shit, he thought. They saved him from jail, only to be put back on the roster as the starting QB, which meant what he feared... Trey would soon be on the move.

But that wasn't a risk, anyway. Right? Like I said, explore, figure out what you want, then scrape him off.

Gryff didn't have to answer to anyone else but himself. Especially not his older brother. But still, Grae must have a reason to keep mentioning that Trey should only be temporary and not forever.

Gryff didn't answer.

Right? came the next text.

While Gryff stared at his phone wondering whether he should bother answering, his phone rang. Somebody had become impatient. He swiped his finger across the screen and reluctantly put it to his ear.

Before he could even get out a greeting, Grae jumped all over him. "Please tell me you're going to scrape him off now. He won't be your client anymore and he'll be busy with this upcoming season. You don't need him in your life. Believe me. He needs to concentrate on being the best damn quarterback out there. Please don't fuck that up."

Gryff's eyebrows knitted, and he frowned. "Are you saying I'll distract him?"

"Yes, that's what I'm saying. Sex tends to do that. He's got a real shot this year to slide that ring on his finger now that this mess is behind him. Don't take that away from him or his teammates."

"If they don't make it to the Super Bowl, it won't be because of me, Grae."

"Good to hear. Break it off soon."

"You assume there's something to break off."

Grae got quiet on the other end of the line.

The hairs on the back of Gryff's neck rose. "What do you know?" he asked softly.

"Only what you told me that day you were at my house."

"Bullshit." Gryff's jaw tightened. "Gia?"

"Her..." Long pause. "And Trey."

"Trey?"

"He came to me for some advice."

Gryff pinched the bridge of his nose and leaned his head back against the backseat of the cab. "What kind of advice?"

"The kind that makes me think there may not be scraping any time soon."

"Big brother—"

"Little brother," Grae countered.

"I got it under control."

"Sure you do. He's not a stray kitten you get to keep."

"Of course he's not a fucking stray kitten." Gryff closed his eyes as a rush of anger rose, and so did his voice. "Why can't I keep him? Who are you to say what I can and cannot do? This doesn't affect you one iota."

Gryff heard Grae's whisper. "Holy shit."

He ignored him. "You do not dictate my sex life. Nor my love life."

"*Fuuuuck.*"

"Shut up," Gryff grumbled.

"You've got it bad, you stupid shit. Bad. And, you're right, this doesn't affect me personally but it might affect the team. I've already explained that."

"I don't give a fuck about the team."

"No, I'm sure you don't. But Trey does. And if you care about him, you'd realize just how important this season is to him."

"To the team," Gryff corrected.

"Them, too. He's been jonesing for a Championship win. This is the team to get there. He is the QB who can get them there *this* season. Don't fuck this up for him. He may not act like it matters, but it does. And it will matter in the end. Down the road, it will matter to him if he loses this chance. He's had a fucked-up life. Let him have this. He's getting to the age where things can go south easily. If it isn't this season, it may not be ever. Do you get what I'm saying?"

Gryff gritted his teeth. "Yes. I get it."

"Good." Grae said softly. "Good. Now let him go. Find someone else. Or just stick with that woman attorney of yours. Concentrate your energy on her."

Gryff rubbed at the sharp pain in his chest. When he went to answer his brother, he realized his phone had gone dark. His brother had hung up on him.

Damn it. He tucked his phone into his suit jacket pocket and scrubbed his face with his palms, then blew out a breath.

There was a shitty saying out there that went something like: if you loved something set it free…

If meant to be, Trey could come back to them after he reached his dream.

Grae was right, neither Gryff nor Rayne should do anything to keep Trey from achieving his goal. They might hold him back without meaning to.

In the meantime, Gryff could move forward with Rayne, because there was no way he would let her go.

He would do whatever he had to do to keep her.

That he could guarantee.

CHAPTER 14

Gryff set his coffee mug down and contemplated the woman who leaned her hip against the counter, arms crossed under her breasts, a spatula in hand, and some eggs frying on the stove.

She wore another one of his T-shirts. This one fell mid-thigh, her smooth legs bare, her painted toes wiggling on the tile floor. Her hair appeared wild but sexy as it fell around her shoulders and down her back.

She stared back at him with a slight curve to her lips.

Her wearing his shirts had become a habit when she stayed over. One he didn't want her to break since he never would have thought a woman could look so good in a man's T-shirt.

But she could pull it off. Especially since her pebbled nipples pressed against the worn cotton.

"Do you think he's awake yet?" she asked.

Gryff tilted his head and listened. He heard nothing but the sound of butter and eggs sizzling in the frying pan.

Gryff answered, "No. If the smell of the bacon in the oven hasn't woken his ass up yet, he may not wake up any time soon."

"Yeah, bacon is his downfall."

"That's why I keep five packs in the freezer now. The man can pack away his pork."

She chuckled at the double entendre, then said, "We could always spend the night at my condo. We don't always have to be here, you know."

"I like you guys here."

"We like to be here, too." She smiled. "Obviously."

He moved behind her and wrapped his arms around her waist, pulling her back against his chest, and pressing his lips into her hair. "I like you wearing my shirts."

"They're comfy."

"It's sexy."

She twisted her head enough to peek up at him over her shoulder. "Really?"

"You can't feel how sexy I think it is?" he whispered in her ear.

"Hmm. I just thought you were excited about the bacon." She sighed softly when he brushed this thumbs over her nipples. "We don't want breakfast to burn."

"Rayne, I need to discuss something with you."

"I'm curious about something, too."

"What?"

"Trey calls me 'baby.' Why don't you?"

Gryff blinked. "Do you want me to?"

"It'd be nice if you... Never mind, Boss."

"So, you want me to give you a special nickname. From my lips to your ears." Gryff grabbed her hair, pulling her head back to drop a big, fat, sloppy kiss on her lips. "Doll."

She elbowed his stomach gently. "No."

He nuzzled the hair by her ear and breathed, "Lover."

She giggled. "No."

"Sweetie."

"No!"

"Mommy."

"Ugh!"

"Oh yeah. That's my favorite. You know you want me to call you Mommy."

"Don't you dare!" she cried out and pulled away from him to flip the eggs over and turn the burner off.

"Oh, yes, *Mommy*."

"Gryff, that's just—"

He burst out laughing and moved away to grab his coffee, taking a healthy swig. "Don't worry, I won't be calling you Mommy in bed. Or anywhere else, for that matter."

"I'm deeply relieved. Could you imagine you calling me that in one of our meetings at the firm?"

"I just wonder if someone would have the balls to question me on it."

"Dani would."

"Probably." He leaned back against the kitchen island. "But seriously, I need to discuss something with you."

"The eggs will get cold."

"I know. Sorry. I don't want to put it off any longer."

Her eyebrows knitted and her expression became cautious. "What?"

"I know you haven't been an associate at the firm very long. But you're my best."

"Then why haven't I moved up to being a senior associate yet?"

Damn. "Rayne, you haven't even been with me—" He shook his head. "My firm for a year yet."

"Is that one of your requirements?"

"You know it is." This had been explained to her during the hiring process. She was just busting his balls.

He hoped.

"Okay," she answered and shrugged.

"But, I have something I want to propose."

Both her expression and her body stilled.

Maybe it was the wrong word to use, but it wasn't far off the mark.

"I want to make you a partner."

"What?" she whispered, her eyes getting wide.

"I want to make you a partner," he repeated, more firmly.

"You don't have any partners."

"If anyone knows that, it's me." He laughed awkwardly. Suddenly, this discussion wasn't going as smoothly as he'd planned. Not that he had given a lot of thought on how to approach Rayne with the idea. He had decided he wanted to make Rayne partner for a variety of reasons. But, he hadn't expected her to be...shocked.

"Boss, I mean... I'm flattered. But, won't it look a bit odd if suddenly the newest associate, not to mention the youngest, who isn't even a senior associate yet, is offered a partnership?"

"It's my firm, my decision."

She made a noise. "I'm well aware of that. Don't you think everyone will say it's because I'm sleeping with the boss?"

"They know your record."

"They aren't going to care. My record might make me a senior associate, then maybe down the road a partner. And I'd need a buy-in. I—" She blew out a breath and shook her head. "I don't think I can afford a buy-in."

"Rayne—"

"No, Gryff. Don't you dare say I don't have to buy in."

"I wasn't going to say that."

"We would split the profits, the bills, the headaches... I don't know if I'm ready for that."

"It's a commitment, that's for sure. But speaking of commitments—"

"Gryff," she whispered, a pained look on her face.

"For fuck's sake, let me get it out first before you make a judgement about what I'm going to say."

She blinked. "Sorry."

He sucked in a breath, staring at her pink polished toes. "I hear your concerns about making partner. I have a solution to that problem."

"What?"

He leveled his gaze at her. "You could..." *Marry me.* "We could..." *Get married.* He swallowed hard. *Fuck.* "I want you to..."

"What? What, Gryff? What are you trying to say?"

He braced himself for what he was about to say. "Marry me, Rayne."

Her eyes widened. "What?"

"If you become my wife, then it won't matter what they say."

"What?" she repeated, looking a bit dazed.

He straightened. Not surprisingly she was in shock. He felt a little shocky, too. He just proposed to someone he had known less than six months, offered to make her a partner in a business he worked long and hard to make the best, and only...*only* just started an intimate relationship with a couple of months ago. And even with that, it was an unconventional one, since it wasn't only the two of them.

He was someone who, once he knew what he wanted, went after it. And he wanted Rayne by his side. As a partner in business, a partner in life.

"Are you aware of what you're asking... offering... I... uh..."

"Yes, I'm pretty aware of what I'm proposing." He certainly *was* well aware of it. He wasn't taking it lightly, either.

"You want her for your *wife?*"

Ah, fuck. Gryff closed his eyes and groaned softly. This was not how he wanted Trey to find out.

He turned toward the entrance to the kitchen to see Trey standing there only wearing a pair of long, loose shorts. Every muscle in his body appeared tight. His jaw clenched. His fingers curled into his palms. His mouth nothing but an angry slash.

"Trey," he said softly, now regretting bringing this up to Rayne before Trey knew his intention.

He meant to talk to him about it.

Sure he did.

He didn't mean to ask her this morning, either. Something

switched in his brain as he watched her putt around his kitchen making them breakfast in his T-shirt.

When something looked right, felt right, it was right.

He hadn't meant to blindside Trey, to hurt him. Though, the other man was seeing it much differently.

He stalked into the kitchen and came toe to toe with Gryff, who stood his ground, even though he felt the anger emanating from Trey's body.

"What the fuck, Gryff? Am I going to be frozen out of this relationship? Am I going to be reduced to a side piece?" He laughed bitterly. "Damn, maybe even not that."

Trey slammed both his palms into Gryff's chest before stepping over to Rayne. He pointed a finger in her face, his own face a mask of fury. "You marry him, I walk."

"Trey," Gryff said softly, trying to keep his own anger at bay. Watching him get in Rayne's face didn't help.

He understood the hurt, the pain he felt. He would have felt betrayed, too.

"No, Gryff. That's some underhanded bullshit right there. Wait. Maybe you want me to walk. Maybe that's what this is all about. You want her for yourself. *Fuck*! I'm such a stupid ass. I should've seen it coming."

"I didn't mean to cut you out."

"Right. So, you two have a nice little ceremony, have someone marry you while this fool," he jabbed his thumb into his chest, "sits in the audience and watches? Cheers you on? Throws bird seed at the end? While you two shove wedding cake into each other's mouths, I should be lucky to catch the crumbs? Fuck that. Fuck that, Gryff. And *fuck you*."

He spun on his heel and took two strides before stopping and shooting Rayne a look. "And fuck you, too, if you say yes."

Then he rushed out of the kitchen, leaving them both in stunned silence for a moment.

Finally, Rayne gave Gryff a wide-eyed look. "Shit."

He agreed. Shit is right.

T rey's head felt like it was about to blow off of his neck. Totally explode like a rocket into space.

He threw his duffel bag on the bed, pulled out a clean pair of jeans, socks, and a T-shirt, then shoved some dirty clothes back in.

Fuck this place. Fuck Gryff. And fuck the fuckery that he heard downstairs.

He fucking proposed to Rayne. Fucking *proposed* to her.

Trey stiffened when he heard Gryff's heavy footsteps approaching. Without turning around, he said, "You fucking want to marry her." He did his best to keep the tremor out of his voice, but he failed.

"Trey," Gryff said softly.

That was all he said. He had no excuses. No explanations. He probably didn't know what to say.

Trey took a shaky breath and shoved his clothes deeper into the bag so he could zip it shut.

He wanted to punch the guy. He really did. But he didn't need to get into more legal trouble. Not that Gryff would call the cops. If Trey popped him one, Gryff should acknowledge he deserved it. Because he did.

Instead, Trey sliced him with his words, wanting him to feel the same pain he felt. The same heartache. "You know, we fuck when you're not around. Did you know that? Did Rayne ever tell you? You won't mind your wife fucking another man?"

Silence greeted him for a moment, then he heard Gryff move closer. Close enough he could feel the other man's body heat. "I'm not trying to cut you out, Trey. I meant to include you in this decision."

"See? *Decision.* The correct word would have been discussion. Not decision."

He tried to wipe the hurt off of his face before he turned toward Gryff. "I'm not your bitch, Gryff. Just because you fuck me doesn't make me your bitch. I'm still a man. A man who plays football, for fuck's sake. You can't get more masculine than that. Just because I let you take me doesn't make you the man and me not. It doesn't work that way in my world. We need to be equal. And not just you and me, but Rayne, too. But you wanting to make her *your* wife leaves me feeling unequal, unwanted and undeserving. Is that what you wanted? Because if so, you've succeeded."

Gryff blew out a breath and curled his fingers around Trey's arm. He looked at the darker hand touching him and yanked his arm from the man's grasp.

"No. You don't get to touch me right now. Maybe not ever."

"I want to make her partner, T."

"T? Now, you want to give me a pet name? *T?* You are something else."

"Sit down."

Trey's brows shot up his face. "Sit down? You're giving me an order right now?"

"Please, T, sit down."

"There you go with that T shit again." Trey shook his head, his heart thumping rapidly in his chest. Panic set in, he could feel it seeping into his skin, his thoughts, his voice. He was going to find himself on his own once again. Not wanted. A burden.

What the fuck.

"If you don't want me, your sister does."

Gryff's spine stiffened. "My sister?"

"Yeah, Gia's been texting me non-stop."

"What the fuck are you talking about?"

"Your sister wants to hook up with me."

"You call her, Trey, and I will pound you into the ground. And I'm not talking about my dick in your ass, either. Stay away from my sister. Now sit down and take a breath."

"You know what gets me? You think you're the leader of this

relationship. That you can dictate what Rayne and I both do, say, feel, whatever. We didn't tap you on the shoulder and tell you you're in charge."

He watched Gryff's body lift, rise, his shoulders straighten. "Trey. Last time I'm telling you. Sit the fuck down and give me a chance to talk to you."

"The talking should have been done before you proposed to Rayne."

"I know. I didn't plan it like that, it just happened."

"Oh, right. *Whoops.* 'Will you marry me?'" Trey moved to the bed and sat down, crossing his arms over his chest, watching through narrowed eyes as Gryff began to pace in front of him, scrubbing a hand over his hair. "You know men can get married now, but you didn't ask me. You know why?"

Gryff's step hesitated when his back was to Trey.

Trey didn't wait for an answer. "Because I'm not good enough to marry, right? I'm not good enough for you."

"We've had this discussion before."

"Yes, and I thought things had changed. That you no longer considered me a spot on your spotless reputation. Especially now that the charges were dropped."

"Of your latest arrest."

Trey sucked in a breath. "Yes, of my latest arrest. Thanks for clarifying that. You're right, it wasn't the only one. So, either you don't want to be with someone with a spotty past or you're afraid I won't be able to stay out of trouble in the future. Which one is it? Or is it both? Be honest."

"Neither."

Trey laughed bitterly and shook his head. "Bullshit. I said to be honest."

Gryff stopped in front of him and met his gaze. There was something in the other man's eyes he couldn't pinpoint. Not anger, not sadness. He wasn't sure what it was.

"I'm being honest. Neither. Do I want you to keep your nose

clean? Yes. Do I think Rayne and I can help you do that? Yes. But..."

"But?"

Gryff's Adam's apple bobbed when he swallowed hard. "You're cleared of your charges, you're back on the roster."

"So?"

"So..." Gryff's chest rose and fell as he inhaled sharply. "So, you'll go do your thing. Get back to training, to throwing a football, go back to what you do best."

"Still not seeing what the problem is? Or what this has to do with you proposing to Rayne. Or why you no longer want me."

Gryff scrubbed his palms over his face and let out a low moan. "I never said I don't want you, T. Okay, in the beginning when I was fighting it. But since then, never. Rayne wants you, I want you. But you'll be gone."

"Gone?"

"Back to the team."

"Okay?"

"You need to concentrate on your career."

Trey shook his head, confused. "There are plenty of players who are married or in committed relationships."

"Yes, but—"

"But nothing. You think because I'm in a relationship with two people instead of one, that my playing will suffer?"

"You want to make it to the Super Bowl."

"Of course. And you think you will hold me back from that? Damn. You're not all that, Gryff." When Gryff gave him a frown, Trey held up a palm. "Okay, yes, you are all that, but not to the point where I can't throw a damn football and can't throw it well. Your dick in my ass does not affect my throwing arm."

"Oh, for fuck's sake."

"Well, isn't that what you're saying?"

"I don't know what I'm trying to say. Maybe I'm just confused. My instinct as a man is to marry Rayne, make her a life partner. Keep her by my side. Normal. You? You're not..."

"A woman."

"Definitely not."

"Not partner material."

"I'm not saying that. But my instinct is different with you."

"You just want to have sex with me, but nothing else."

"No."

"Then what?"

Gryff blew out a loud breath. "I'm not sure how to handle all of this."

"You like to be in control and suddenly your life has spun out of control. You don't know how to right your world. So, you proposed to Rayne to bring some normality back into your life. Into your abnormal relationship. I'm starting to understand."

"I'm glad someone is."

"But you still want to marry Rayne."

"Yes."

"Do you still want me in your life? Yours and Rayne's?"

"Yes. Fuck yes. Yes! Damn it."

"Okay. So, again, what's the problem?"

"I don't know how to make it…" Gryff's voice drifted off.

"Neat."

Gryff dropped to his knees at Trey's feet with his hands on Trey's thighs and looked up. "Yes. Neat. I'm afraid because this is so messy, that it will screw up your chances at being the best football player you can be."

"It's not messy for me, Gryff, that's the thing. It's only messy in your head. Not mine."

Gryff's lips flattened.

"I'd be perfectly happy if all of us eventually moved in together. None of us need a wedding band to be a part of each other's life."

"You mean you'd want for us all to live together?" Gryff asked, almost as if surprised at the suggestion.

"Well, wouldn't you expect Rayne to move in if she agreed to marry you? You'd live together. Then there would be me. Do you just

JEANNE ST. JAMES

expect me to come over every once in a while? Get your rocks off, then I go home afterward and let you and Rayne get on with your married life? Or are you expecting me to become bored being in a relationship and drift away eventually? Go on to my next fling."

"What do you want, T?"

"What do I want? Ah, fuck." He sucked in a deep breath in preparation of laying it all out. "I want you to call me T. I want you to fuck me whenever and wherever you want to. I want you to eventually let me top you." He lifted a hand before Gryff could argue that point. "No rush. I can wait. I want to fall asleep every night with you and Rayne. I want to kiss you both goodbye every morning as you head to the office and I head in for practice. I want to come home late from practice or home from an away game and know you kept dinner warm for me. *Jesus.*" Trey's breath hitched as reality hit him. "I guess I want domestic bliss. Trey Holloway wants to be tied down. And not in the kinky way. Though, that would be nice once in a while, too."

"You want to be tied down," Gryff repeated, sounding amused.

"And tied up. Don't forget that part."

Gryff's eyes crinkled at the corners and his lips twitched. "You have to promise me something."

"Keep my nose clean. You've beat that into me already."

"No. Well, yes, that, too."

"Then what?"

"Get that Super Bowl ring."

Trey smiled and nodded. He was all over that promise. He not only wanted it, he could taste it. This would be his year. Especially with two people who he cared about and who cared about him at his back.

EPILOGUE

"**F**uck you, Trey." Rayne heard as she headed toward the family room.

Her lips twisted into a smile at Trey's response. "I love you, too, boss man."

Gryff groaned. "We are not watching this *again*."

Trey dropped a bowl of popcorn in Gryff's lap before leaping over the couch and landing on his ass with a bounce. "Oh, look at that landing. Perfect score. Ten points. Oh! And the crowd roars. Raaaaaaar!"

"What did I tell you about jumping on the couch?" Rayne asked, holding two fresh beers for her men.

"Yes, Mommy," Trey teased, sounding like a scolded child, then turned to Gryff. "It's been a while since we've watched it."

Gryff snorted and accepted one of the beers. "Yeah, like since last weekend. It's getting old."

"It will never get old."

"Says you."

"Why? What are we watching?" Rayne looked up at the large flat screen that hung on the wall. She grimaced. "Oh shit."

"Yeah. Exactly."

"No. We were supposed to be watching a movie of my choice," she complained, shoving the remaining beer at Trey.

"We are not watching some chick flick. Us men want to watch this again."

"Speak for yourself," Gryff grumbled.

Trey cocked an eyebrow at Gryff. "You'd rather watch *Beaches* again?"

He frowned. "Hell no."

"That's not what I picked."

"Okay," Trey said. "*Twilight* then."

"Right, like I'd watch that," she said, tapping both men on their knees so they'd make room for her in the middle of the couch.

"Wait. Did you draw the straw for the middle?"

"I don't need a straw. I get the middle," she said, squeezing between them in the small space they made. Gryff wrapped an arm around her shoulders, tucking her into his side. She fit perfectly.

"Oooh. I love it when you're bossy," Trey claimed, wiggling his eyebrows.

Rayne laughed. "*You* do. This one not so much," she said tilting her head toward Gryff.

"I'm the boss, remember?" Gryff said, reaching over her in an attempt to snag the remote out of Trey's hand. Trey lifted it up and out of his reach.

"Whoever has the remote is the boss."

Rayne plucked the remote out of Trey's fingers when he wasn't expecting it. "Okay, then that settles it."

"See?" Trey asked. "Bossy."

"Yes, because I'm not sitting through this whole game again. We've watched it a million times," she answered.

"Not that many."

"Close enough."

"Can we just watch the fourth quarter?"

Gryff groaned. "By now, I can quote the sportscasters through the whole damn game."

"Okay, just the final five minutes."

"Five minutes' real time or game time?" Gryff asked. "Because five minutes of game time feels like a damn hour."

Trey sighed. "I can compromise. Let's just watch the ceremony afterward."

Rayne chuckled. "So we can see you make out with the Lombardi trophy again? You left tongue marks on it."

"It's sexy." Trey settled his arm around her shoulders, too. "Like you, baby."

Having her men cuddle her on the couch made her heart swell. She loved them both so much. And she felt loved. Very loved.

"It was so unsanitary and gross. So many fingers touching it. *Blech.*"

"It was worth it. Fast forward to the ceremony. Please. Yeah, there. When the confetti was raining down."

Rayne and Gryff might complain about watching the Super Bowl game from last February over and over again. But when it came to the ceremony, Rayne always had to fight back the tears. And, honestly, she could never get enough of watching the pure joy and sense of pride on Trey's face when they handed him the trophy to hold over his head. And, yes, he did French kiss it in his excitement.

She and Gryff had watched the game from the Bulldog's suite along with Grae, Paige and Connor, and what seemed like a hundred other people. Rayne had chewed off all her nails by the third quarter.

Gryff had almost punched a wall when Trey threw an interception in the fourth quarter. Her? She almost puked, so there was that.

They were all in tears during the last few seconds of the game. With a tied score, Trey threw a bomb that gave them the win, made him the MVP, and brought the Lombardi trophy home to Boston.

Then he decided to hang up his cleats since he had achieved his dream.

Rayne noticed the part of the tape where Gryff and she joined him on camera. Trey wasn't shy about hugging Rayne tightly to his side, planting a big kiss on her lips, before sneaking an arm around Gryff's waist while being interviewed by rabid sports reporters.

She didn't have to see the tape to remember the pride in Gryff's eyes, the larger than life smile on his face.

Questions followed on their relationship. And, of course, the gossip rags made up all kinds of outrageous claims. They ignored it all. Even Grae had helped run interference.

Once the cameras panned away from Trey, Rayne shut the recording off. Before she could switch on a movie, Trey grabbed the remote and put it on the coffee table.

"I have something to tell you guys."

Gryff leaned forward and placed the popcorn bowl on the table, too. Then he twisted to face the two of them. "This should be good."

Rayne patted his thigh, and he snagged her hand, intertwining his long, dark fingers with hers. He gave her hand a squeeze.

Trey twisted in his seat, too, a small smile on his face.

"Okay, T, let's hear it," Gryff said gruffly.

"I decided to go back to school."

Rayne's mouth gaped, and she felt Gryff shift next to her.

"You already have a degree."

"Yeah, but watching you and Rayne be partners in the firm, I kind of feel left out."

Rayne started to protest, but Trey lifted a hand to stop her. "I will be thirty-three soon. I can't stay home and be a househusband. Though, a hot, sexy one wearing a Super Bowl ring. Not many can say that," he teased. "But you two go off every morning, have a purpose. I have none." He pinned his gaze on Gryff. "When you proposed to Rayne all those months ago, you said you wanted her to be a partner, not only in business but in life. I get it now."

"And what does this have to do with school?" Gryff prodded him.

"Not just any school. Law school."

"What? Really?" Rayne asked, surprised. "That's great!"

"I just figured you'd rather lounge around like a kept man," Gryff said. Though he said it seriously, there was a twinkle in his eyes, and his lips twitched.

"I want to get my law degree, join you two at the firm."

"We have a tough hiring process. The interview alone is brutal," Gryff said.

Rayne rolled her eyes at Gryff and then smiled at Trey. "You can intern with me."

"Oh wait. What? No." Gryff said. "You two won't get any work done. No. He can intern with Maggie."

Maggie, being one of the most unattractive women in the office, though, an excellent attorney. Rayne shook her head. "That means he can join the firm."

"I didn't say that. I said we'd have to interview him first."

Trey snorted. "Okay, I'll do whatever I need to do. But, first I need to get through school. Does interning pay?"

"No," Gryff answered at the same time Rayne said, "Yes."

He was just busting Trey's balls. She fought back her smile.

"Whatever. I don't need the money. Not only am I a World Champion, I'm a kept man." He smirked.

"Whatever, T," Gryff echoed. "You have more money than Rayne and I combined. Especially after selling your penthouse. And you have your endorsement deals. Not to mention that sweet little bonus you got for the Super Bowl win."

"That bonus money has already been spent."

Gryff frowned, "On what?"

"Something for the three of us."

It was Rayne's turn to frown. "What are you talking about?"

"I wanted to surprise you."

"For fuck's sake, T, get to the point."

"Jesus, so demanding. Well..." He gave them a Cheshire cat smile. "Well, since I've had time on my hands while you two are heading off to bring home the bacon, I decided..." His voice drifted off.

"Trey," Gryff warned.

"To hire a planner to plan..." He hesitated again.

Gryff looked at the ceiling and muttered, "Holy fuck."

"Our commitment ceremony."

Gryff's gaze bounced to Trey, Rayne, then landed back on Trey. "Our what?"

"You wanted to marry Rayne. You two decided to not do that because of me. I appreciate that. I love the both of you. I want all three of us to be committed."

"We are," Rayne said, surprised at this turn of events. She had no clue what Trey had been planning. How he kept it a secret with his exuberance, she'd never know.

"I was talking to Grae."

"Oh fuck."

"And he told me about the ceremony that Paige's brother Logan had with his partners, Ty and Quinn."

"So?"

"So, then he told me about the ceremony that Renny, Cole and Eve had."

"They all have children," Gryff stated.

"You don't want a ceremony? You don't want something that commits the three of us together?"

"Do *you* want a ceremony?" Rayne asked. "I don't need one. I doubt Gryff needs one. But if *you* want one, I'm not against it. Gryff?"

His answer completely floored her. "Yes. I want one, too. I think it's a good idea."

Trey laughed. "Holy shit, boss man thinks one of my ideas is good. Write this date down. I need to remember it."

"Very funny. No, you're right, T. I think a small ceremony would be nice to have for our family and our closest friends."

"Our closest one thousand friends?"

"No. No more than fifty."

"Damn. I wanted it to be a big shindig."

"No. I will agree to it if it's small and intimate. Rayne?"

"I agree. Nothing crazy," she answered.

"So, we're doing this?"

Gryff nodded and said softly, his voice full of warmth, "Yeah, we can do this."

"Yes, if you need something to show people that we love each other, then I'm fine with it. In fact, the idea is growing on me," Rayne said, picturing herself standing between her men at an altar surrounded with beautiful lilies, exchanging vows and rings. Being introduced to their friends and family as a committed threesome.

Yes, she could picture that very clearly.

Plus, it would prove to Trey that they were committed to him. And him to them. He's found his forever home, his forever family. His partners in life.

To show that there was no doubt that he was wanted and loved. That they were each other's in all ways.

Rayne patted both their thighs, feeling a sting in her eyes. She sniffled. "Okay, enough with this mushy stuff. Let's watch The Notebook."

Gryff groaned. "Oh, for fuck's sake. Not that movie again."

Trey yelled, "Fuck no. Last time I went through a whole damn box of tissues. My man card was revoked for a full month."

She giggled and scrolled through the movies. She settled on an action flick instead that made her men feel like men and her feeling lucky to be cuddled in between them.

Life was *good*.

∼

Sign up for Jeanne's newsletter to learn about her upcoming releases, sales and more! http://www.jeannestjames.com/ newslettersignup

∼

Turn the page for a sneak peek of Book 5 of the Dare Menage

Series: Dare to Surrender

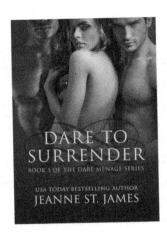

One woman, two men, a fierce attraction and a danger that could destroy them all...

Olivia Holloway's life has never been easy. On her own at sixteen, she's fought to survive ever since. When she finds herself in a dangerous situation that even she can't handle, she has to break down and ask for help. She reluctantly seeks it by showing up at her estranged brother's law firm. However, it's not her brother, Trey, who steps in, it's the firm's private investigator, Elliot Stone and his husband, Grant Lane. They agree to hide her at their home to keep her safe after she witnesses a powerful Senator commit murder.

Together for a decade, Eli and Grant's marriage is solid and they're still deeply in love. But when Olivia shows up at the firm they both work at, Eli feels a pull toward the woman he can't deny. Only now he needs to convince his husband that bringing her into their relationship will not destroy what they have but only enhance it. However, will Grant agree?

And will the trouble that's following Olivia put them all at risk?

DARE TO SURRENDER

CHAPTER 1

Olivia could hear nothing but the pounding of her heart in her ears. She stared at the large gold letters on the wall above the reception desk... *Ward, Jordan, & Holloway.*

The receptionist's lips were moving but Liv had no idea what the woman said.

She needed to turn and hightail it out of there before she got caught. This was a bad idea. One of way too many she'd made in her life.

Her stomach churned, and her mouth felt like it was packed full of cotton.

She closed her eyes for a moment, as a wave of panic washed up and over her. She could fix this herself. She'd been surviving on her own most of her life.

She never needed anyone to save her, and she didn't now.
Right.

She stiffened when she felt something, or someone, large and very warm at her back. She shook her head in an attempt to clear it and finally heard, "Are you okay?"

So, unless the receptionist had a deep, masculine voice, it wasn't a woman. A shiver ran down her spine.

When a large dark hand landed on her arm, she could only stare at it. She blinked. Why was this person touching her?

Then fingers wrapped around her chin, lifting her face and her gaze. She stared into very, very dark eyes. Eyes full of concern and... something else.

She wasn't used to the concern. That look seemed foreign to her. And the other? She had no clue why he would look at her like that.

"What?" she whispered, almost as if trapped in a fog.

"Are you okay?" The man snapped into motion, leading her over to a nearby chair and pushing her gently into it. "Cassie, grab a bottle of water."

From the corner of her eye, she saw the receptionist move at a hurried pace.

"Are you okay?"

Why did he keep asking her that?

"Yes," she murmured, her tongue thick.

"Are you here to see someone in particular?"

Liv watched his dark lips move. They were full and looked nice. And his teeth were really white. Nice people had nice lips, nice voices, and nice teeth.

Why did she care if he was nice?

"Yes."

"Who? Who do you have an appointment with?"

Liv shook her head slowly. "I don't."

"Then who are you here to see?"

She sucked in a shaky breath. "Trey."

"Trey," he echoed softly.

"Yes, Trey Holloway."

He tilted his head, his gaze searching her face. "Does he know you?"

What a weird question. "I hope so. He's my brother."

His dark eyes narrowed, and he only left her long enough to grab the bottle of water from Cassie, the receptionist. He cracked the seal on the lid and opened it, handing the bottle to her. "Drink."

"I'm not thirsty," she said, her tone flat, even though she felt parched.

"Drink anyway."

Liv lifted the bottle to her lips and sipped at the cool water. She blinked again and glanced up at the man towering over her. "Who are you?"

"Eli."

"Eli," Liv repeated, frowning, still feeling as if in a daze.

"Elliott Stone."

That was a nice name for someone with nice features. Some men didn't look right being bald. He did. His head was perfectly smooth and nicely shaped. Bald fit him. "Elliott," she repeated.

"Yes. Let me get Trey for you." He stepped back and turned to leave.

"No!"

He stopped, his back straightening. He was tall. Dark. And oh-so handsome. But, right now, none of that mattered.

Nothing mattered but why she was here.

Though, she should really leave before her brother was dragged into her mess. Especially since she hadn't seen him in sixteen years.

Because of that, he might not be happy with her. She had disappeared without a trace. No calls, no letters, no emails. She had gotten lost. Completely disappeared. And left him behind to deal with what was their nightmare of a childhood.

So, it was a bad idea for her to show up here in her moment of weakness.

"No. I'm just going to leave. I'll catch up with him another time. I thank you for your kindness." She pushed to her feet and beelined toward the lobby elevator.

He snagged her elbow as she passed and swung her around until they came face to face, his eyes dark and searching. "Whoa. No. You're not going anywhere."

She jerked her elbow, but his grip was tight enough that she couldn't pull free. "You can't tell me what to do."

"The hell I can't," he mumbled close to her ear. "You know why? Because I've worked here for a while now and never knew Trey had a sister. And now I'm wondering why I never knew that. So, to satisfy my curiosity, I'll escort you back to his office."

"Get your hand off me," she snapped, still tugging her arm.

"You didn't say please."

Right now, she didn't think he was so nice. "Please," she said with a forced nicety.

"That's better. But no."

She looked in panic toward the receptionist who just gave her a blank stare in return, like the woman was used to seeing large men dragging women through the lobby. Liv couldn't imagine it happened on a regular basis. But she'd seen a lot of crazy shit in her life, so nothing would surprise her.

"Let's go," he said, a determined look on his face.

Liv tried to dig her heels into the nice carpeting, but he was too big and too strong to resist. She hardly got a glimpse of the various offices they passed until he abruptly stopped in front of another woman. A secretary maybe.

"Trey in?"

The woman's eyes bounced to Liv before landing on this bossy Elliott, giving him a big, flirty smile.

Whatever.

"He's not in his office. He's in a meeting."

"A *real* meeting or a *meeting*."

Liv had no idea what he was getting at, but it made her glance up at him. He ignored her.

"Uh. I would hope just a regular meeting since Grant's in with them. Because if it's not a regular meeting, you may have to step in." Then the secretary giggled.

Which was strange. Liv had no idea why what she said was funny.

Elliott frowned, and his already dark face got darker. "Then it's a regular meeting."

"If you say so," she murmured, then gave him another bright smile. "Large conference room."

Elliott, Eli, or whatever, gave the woman a sharp nod and dragged Liv down another hallway to a long room made up by a wall of windows. Several people sat around a long oval conference table and as he approached with his hand firmly on her elbow, all heads swung toward them.

He must have communicated something silently through the glass because a large black man got up and opened the door just as they hit the threshold.

"What's going on?" the large man asked, frowning.

Ignoring him, Elliott dragged her into the room, asking Liv's brother, "This belong to you?"

With wide eyes they stared at each other.

"I think so," Trey murmured, studying her hard.

"You think, or you know?"

Trey Holloway stood and looked at her from head to toe. "Yeah. She's my sister. *Damn.*"

"I found her skulking around the lobby in a state of panic," her captor announced to the room of strangers.

Her gaze shot up to him. "What? I wasn't skulk—"

"Quiet," this Elliott said sharply, cutting her off.

"Eli, you want to let her go?" the fourth man at the end of the table asked, slowly rising to his feet.

"She might run."

"What?" Trey asked, his eyebrows shooting to his hairline.

"She tried to take off."

"Why?"

Eli shrugged his broad shoulders and glanced down at her for a moment before saying, "I don't know. You'll have to ask her."

Liv frowned. "I'm right here. I can hear you and I'm quite capable of answering."

Eli shrugged again and finally released her elbow. As she rubbed it, her gaze drifted over everyone in the room.

Her brother looked good. Mature. Important. But then, he'd been a star quarterback for the Boston Bulldogs and helped them win the Super Bowl Championship a couple of seasons ago.

A woman with long strawberry blonde hair watched her with curious eyes. When she stood, Liv couldn't help but notice the sexy way she was dressed. Pencil skirt, stockings, and heels that were high, not as high as stripper heels, but they made her legs look endless. Liv's gaze landed on her chest. She certainly had plenty there. The woman moved next to Trey and placed a hand on her brother's back.

Liv found that curious.

And when the woman said something softly to her brother, he seemed to snap to attention like he'd just woken up. As he moved forward, Liv thought he was going to grab her into a bear hug, but then he froze and looked at her cautiously.

"Olivia, what are you doing here?"

Coming here was not a good idea. "What? I can't stop in and say hello to my brother?" Her teasing fell flat.

"It's been sixteen years."

And there it was. The one sentence that brought all the guilt she'd been carrying around with her to the forefront. Heat rushed into her cheeks as all eyes pinned on her. "I... uh..."

"Baby, maybe we should clear out and let them have a moment."

Liv spun to the man at her right. He was also tall, but not as tall as Eli. He had a nice tan, and very kind, warm hazel eyes behind glasses that made him look highly intelligent. But she wondered who he called baby, since the only other woman in the room had now clung to the only other black man in the room. The one who seemed to be in charge. Liv found it strange that the woman took liberties like that with both men.

"Grant, they may need me," Eli answered him.

This Grant called Eli "baby?" Elliott Stone did not look like someone who would let another man call him that endearment, especially in a professional setting. Weird.

"I'm sure if they need you, they'll let you know." Grant looked at Trey, who only nodded in answer. "See? We can wait in my office until they're done."

"Yes, but—"

"Eli," the man said firmly to her former captor with an undertone that clearly meant not to question him.

Eli nodded and then sighed. He leaned toward Liv. "We're not done."

Liv pulled all the bravado she could gather and said, "Oh, we're done," matter-of-factly.

His wide lips flattened, and he reluctantly followed the other man, who Liv assumed was another attorney since he wore a suit, out the door. They shut it behind him.

Then there were only four. Her, her brother, and the other two.

"Why now?" Trey asked.

She wondered why the other two didn't excuse themselves. She purposely avoided looking at them when she asked, "Can we speak privately?"

His eyes flicked to the large black man, then the blonde woman before saying, "No. Anything you have to say can be said in front of Rayne and Gryff."

Rayne and Gryff.

"They're my partners," he clarified, then added, "in all things."

In all things? What did that mean?

The man who had to be Gryff said, "We can give you two a few moments alone, T."

"No, stay. I want you to stay," Trey answered. Without turning around, he reached his arm back and they touched hands briefly, then dropped them.

"So again, why and why now?" Trey asked.

"No hug for your baby sister?" Liv asked, which even sounded lame to her ears. She was stalling.

Something flashed behind his eyes. "Really? You disappear at sixteen, show up sixteen years later and I'm supposed to act like it was just yesterday that I saw you? You left me behind."

Liv closed her eyes and inhaled a shaky breath. "I know."

"Not even a peep. Not once. Not when I graduated high school. Not when I went off to college. Not when our *lovely* mother died. Not when I was drafted into the NFL. Not when I won the fucking Super Bowl."

The last part sounded bitter and raw. Liv watched various emotions cross his features. "I'm sorry," she whispered. "I was just trying to survive. I did what I had to do."

"Yeah, so did I."

Liv looked at him in surprise at his tone, wondering what he had to do to survive. Whatever he had to do, it seemed he had come out on the winning end.

Gryff moved forward, laying a hand on Trey's shoulder. "Look, you both did what you had to do. It was your mother who was to blame. T, don't lay that on your sister's shoulders. She was an innocent like you in the whole thing."

Maybe the man was an ally.

"Which one of you is Jordan and which one is Ward?"

The stunning woman came forward with a smile and held out her hand. "I'm Rayne Jordan. And that's Gryffin Ward."

Liv took her hand tentatively, but Rayne shook it firmly and with respect. She raised her gaze from their clasped hands to her face, blinked at how green the other woman's eyes were and then gave her a small smile. "I'm Olivia Holloway."

"I gathered that. Why don't you have a seat?" Rayne swept a hand toward one of the many empty chairs that looked expensive but comfortable.

"I... uh..."

Gryff pulled out a nearby chair and also indicated that she should sit. She sat. Then her brother and his partners moved to the other side of the table and settled across from her.

Liv cleared her throat since she suddenly felt as though she was on trial. "I'm sorry for coming here unexpectedly."

"You're family. No need to apologize," Gryff said, his expression blank.

Family? Yes, to Trey. But...

She slid her gaze to her brother. "Trey."

"Yes?"

"I... uh. I need help."

"Yeah, I didn't think you showed up because you missed me."

Once again, heat crawled up Liv's throat to flood her cheeks. "Sorry, I shouldn't have bothered you."

She rolled back her chair and before she could stand, a loud, deep voice commanded, "Stay."

"Boss," Rayne murmured.

Gryff didn't take his eyes off Liv. "No, she came here for a reason. We need to hear why."

Boss? She thought they were partners.

"Olivia," Gryff started.

"Liv. Please, call me Liv."

"Fine. Liv, no matter what, we're family."

Her eyebrows furrowed. "I don't understand how we're family."

The three across from her looked at each other and then back to her. Trey finally said, "These are my partners, Liv."

"Okay, I get that. I saw your last names in big gold letters over the receptionist's desk."

Trey took a deep breath. "We're committed life partners, too."

Liv blinked, then stared at her brother. Committed life partners. What did that mean?

Oh shit.

"All three of you?"

He nodded.

"Oh."

"So, as much as I'm enjoying this little family reunion, can you tell me why you're coming to me now after all these years?"

"I... uh."

"Oh, for fuck's sake," the large man across from her muttered, his hands flexing on the table.

"Gryff," Rayne said softly. "Give her a chance."

Liv's eyes slid to Rayne, to Gryff, then back to her brother. "I... I shouldn't be here."

Her brother was happy, settled, successful. She didn't need to be dragging him into her mess.

She could do this on her own. She could.

Fuck. She couldn't.

She had no one who she could trust. She had nowhere to go. This was it. She had no choice.

"I need help."

"You said that," Trey said, his eyebrows pulled low. "Legal help?"

"Yes... No..." She shook her head. It was all so freaking confusing. "I don't know."

"You don't know?" Gryff asked, frowning.

"I'm in trouble."

Gryff leaned back in his chair, his arms stretched out, his palms flat on the table in front of him. "No shit."

It was not a good idea to come here. It wasn't. She needed to leave. She had no right to ask her brother for help. She had no right to intrude in his life. He owed her nothing.

"I'm sorry," she whispered, meeting her brother's eyes. He had the exact same eyes as her. The same color hair. They looked so much alike but were complete strangers.

"Don't be sorry," Rayne said softly. "Talk to us. We can help."

"I'm not so sure about that."

"Then why did you come here?" Trey asked.

"Because I have nowhere else to go." The words spilled out of her in a rush. They were true, but she hated to admit it.

"You found a place to go sixteen years ago," her brother said softly, the hurt evident in his voice.

Liv closed her eyes and sucked in a breath. "I had nowhere to go then, either."

"Are you going to get to the point or are you going to continue to jerk our chains?" Gryff finally said.

"Boss," Rayne murmured softly. Her hand slid over to cover one of his.

His eyes dropped to study them then lifted back to Liv. "We can't help you if you don't tell us what the problem is."

She opened her mouth, closed it, then opened it again. Even if they couldn't help, she needed to get this off her chest. She sucked in another breath. "I witnessed a murder."

Deafening silence greeted her from around the table. She stared at her own clasped hands, afraid to see their expressions.

"Just go to the police and tell them what you witnessed," Trey said like he heard that confession every day.

If it was only that simple. "I can't do that."

"Why?" Gryff asked, his deep voice now tinged with suspicion.

"Because of who was involved," she told the table.

"Fuck," Gryff grumbled.

"Who was involved?" Rayne asked softly.

She was afraid to even say his name. "Randall Dean," she whispered, fear shooting through her. If anyone overheard her, found out what she knew, what she saw...

Rayne sucked in a sharp breath, and Gryff made a noise. Liv glanced up at Trey, who was shaking his head, looking confused. "Who?"

Gryff shot Trey a look. "Randall Dean," he repeated, as if that would clear up her brother's confusion.

"I have no fucking clue who that is," Trey answered.

"He was involved?" Gryff asked, leaning forward, his body tense.

"Yes," Liv answered.

"How?"

"He killed her." God, he killed Peggy.

"Who?"

A woman who was making changes to her life, a life she was

trying to improve. Liv knew exactly what that was like. She had been in her shoes once. "A woman I knew."

"How do you know it was him?"

He freaking wrapped his hands around her throat until all the life was squeezed out of her. "I saw him do it."

"Fuck!" Gryff barked to the ceiling. He grabbed the phone on the center of the conference table and jerked it toward him. He picked up the handset, jabbed some numbers and then growled, "Eli, in here, now," then slammed down the phone.

"Holy shit," Rayne murmured. She sent worried eyes Liv's direction. "Are you sure?"

"Yes." Hell yes, she was sure. She'd never forget what she saw. Not ever. That was burned into her brain and would be for the rest of her life.

"So why can't she go to the police?" Trey asked, still confused.

The conference room door was yanked open and her former captor stepped in, closing the door, eyes locked on her. Suddenly the room had so much less oxygen. She was finding it hard to breathe.

"Are you okay?" Rayne asked, concern lacing her voice.

No, no she wasn't.

She had pushed what she saw from her mind, trying only to think about how she could escape, how she could save herself. Once again, how she could survive.

Suddenly, everything was coming crashing down on her all over again.

And having this big man standing next to her, dark, intense eyes pinning her in her chair didn't help.

"Boss," Eli grumbled.

"Sit down," Gryff said.

"I'm fine..."

He needed to sit down. To give her space. "Please," Liv croaked. "Please."

Eli looked at her, his dark eyebrows furrowed. But he finally moved to the chair down from her, leaving an empty seat between them. For that, she was thankful.

Something about his presence overwhelmed her, and she wouldn't be able to talk, to answer questions, with him looming over her.

"What's going on?" Eli asked, his eyes flicking from her to Gryff back to her.

"She saw a Randall Dean kill someone," Trey said from the other end of the table.

Eli's gaze swung his direction. "What?"

"Do you know who he is?" her brother asked.

"Holy fuck," Eli breathed.

"Right," Gryff grunted.

"This is a mess," Rayne added.

Eli held up a hand. "Hold up. We need to rewind, and I need to hear this from the beginning."

"I think we all do," Gryff agreed.

Then all eyes landed on her. *Shit.*

Get it here: Dare to Surrender

IF YOU ENJOYED THIS BOOK

Thank you for reading A Daring Desire. If you enjoyed Gryff, Rayne, and Trey's story, please consider leaving a review at your favorite book retailer and/or Goodreads to let other readers know. Reviews are always appreciated and just a few words can help an independent author like me tremendously!

ALSO BY JEANNE ST. JAMES

Find my complete reading order here:
https://www.jeannestjames.com/reading-order

* Available in Audiobook

Standalone Books:

Made Maleen: A Modern Twist on a Fairy Tale *

Damaged *

Rip Cord: The Complete Trilogy *

Everything About You (A Second Chance Gay Romance) *

Reigniting Chase (An M/M Standalone) *

Brothers in Blue Series:

Brothers in Blue: Max *

Brothers in Blue: Marc *

Brothers in Blue: Matt *

Teddy: A Brothers in Blue Novelette *

Brothers in Blue: A Bryson Family Christmas *

The Dare Ménage Series:

Double Dare *

Daring Proposal *

Dare to Be Three *

A Daring Desire *

Dare to Surrender *

A Daring Journey *

The Obsessed Novellas:

Forever Him *

Only Him *

Needing Him *

Loving Her *

Tempting Him *

Down & Dirty: Dirty Angels MC Series®:

Down & Dirty: Zak *

Down & Dirty: Jag *

Down & Dirty: Hawk *

Down & Dirty: Diesel *

Down & Dirty: Axel *

Down & Dirty: Slade *

Down & Dirty: Dawg *

Down & Dirty: Dex *

Down & Dirty: Linc *

Down & Dirty: Crow *

Crossing the Line (A DAMC/Blue Avengers MC Crossover) *

Magnum: A Dark Knights MC/Dirty Angels MC Crossover *

Crash: A Dirty Angels MC/Blood Fury MC Crossover *

In the Shadows Security Series:

Guts & Glory: Mercy *

Guts & Glory: Ryder *

Guts & Glory: Hunter *

Guts & Glory: Walker *

Guts & Glory: Steel *

Guts & Glory: Brick *

Blood & Bones: Blood Fury MC®:

Blood & Bones: Trip *

Blood & Bones: Sig *

Blood & Bones: Judge *

Blood & Bones: Deacon *

Blood & Bones: Cage *

Blood & Bones: Shade *

Blood & Bones: Rook *

Blood & Bones: Rev *

Blood & Bones: Ozzy

Blood & Bones: Dodge

Blood & Bones: Whip

Blood & Bones: Easy

Beyond the Badge: Blue Avengers MC™:

Beyond the Badge: Fletch

Beyond the Badge: Finn

Beyond the Badge: Decker

Beyond the Badge: Rez

Beyond the Badge: Crew

Beyond the Badge: Nox

COMING SOON!

Double D Ranch (An MMF Ménage Series)

Dirty Angels MC®: The Next Generation

WRITING AS J.J. MASTERS

The Royal Alpha Series:

(A gay mpreg shifter series)

The Selkie Prince's Fated Mate *

The Selkie Prince & His Omega Guard *

The Selkie Prince's Unexpected Omega *

The Selkie Prince's Forbidden Mate *

The Selkie Prince's Secret Baby *

ABOUT THE AUTHOR

JEANNE ST. JAMES is a USA Today bestselling romance author who loves an alpha male (or two). She was only thirteen when she started writing and her first paid published piece was an erotic story in Playgirl magazine. Her first romance novel, Banged Up, was published in 2009. She is happily owned by farting French bulldogs. She writes M/F, M/M, and M/M/F ménages.

Want to read a sample of her work? Download a sampler book here: BookHip.com/MTQQKK

To keep up with her busy release schedule check her website at www.jeannestjames.com or sign up for her newsletter: http://www. jeannestjames.com/newslettersignup

www.jeannestjames.com
jeanne@jeannestjames.com

Newsletter: http://www.jeannestjames.com/newslettersignup
Jeanne's Down & Dirty Book Crew: https://www.facebook.com/ groups/JeannesReviewCrew/
TikTok: https://www.tiktok.com/@jeannestjames

facebook.com/JeanneStJamesAuthor

amazon.com/author/jeannestjames

instagram.com/JeanneStJames

bookbub.com/authors/jeanne-st-james

goodreads.com/JeanneStJames

pinterest.com/JeanneStJames